ALICE CROMIE

# Nobody Wanted to Scare Her

ILLUSTRATED
BY JULIE BRINCKLOE

*Doubleday & Company, Inc., Garden City, New York*

With special acknowledgments to Ralph Newman, Paul Angle, Bell I. Wiley and T. Harry Williams.

LIBRARY OF CONGRESS CATALOGING IN PUBLICATION DATA

Cromie, Alice Hamilton.
   Nobody wanted to scare her.

   SUMMARY: Many people seem interested in obtaining possession of the mysterious box that twelve-year-old Gillian is charged with delivering to her guardian in Europe.
   [1. Mystery and detective stories] I. Brinckloe, Julie, illus. II. Title.
PZ7.C878No    [Fic]
ISBN 0-385-02845-8 TRADE
       0-385-05403-3 PREBOUND
LIBRARY OF CONGRESS CATALOG CARD NUMBER 73–20723

*To Bob and Howard and Rod and Doc*

# Nobody Wanted to Scare Her

# 1

Gillian had been an orphan for so long she seldom thought about it. This fourth year, almost never. Not until this afternoon.

An hour ago Jojo's suite in the Goldcoast East hotel on Chicago's rich north side had seemed the safest and busiest place in the world. Then Jojo, who was the oldest and usually the most dependable of her guardians, had told his staff they'd better get a move on if they wanted to make it to California. Chicago was in for the granddad of all summer storms, he said, and he didn't want to wear himself out waiting at O'Hare Airport for wings west.

That must have been what got her to thinking about relatives, real ones—who could be counted on in any weather, any time, any place.

She had been thirteen since the end of May and that made her feel grown up most days, though not today. She was still flatter and bonier than her best and sometimes worst friend and roommate at school, Mary Agatha Pierce, but she was taller than Mary Ag. Her hair was straight, though a month at camp had streaked it from light brown to bone-colored. Her eyes were green as her father's had been, not black and snapping and reading-you-too-clearly like Jojo's.

Jojo was Jordan James. He was a movie actor nowadays and a poet and a singer, but nearly everyone still thought of him as "The Black Comet" of pro football, or as old No. 23, the best twice-All-American halfback Midwest University ever had.

Her other guardians were Budd Greenburg and Cory Moore, who were almost as busy as Jojo. Budd was European editor for a very important publisher. He could translate books from four languages and he had an apartment in Paris. Cory was a sportswriter for the Chicago *Tribune*, as Gillian's father had been. His by-line read Corydon Moore and he also reviewed books and liked all kinds of museums and once had a hole-in-one at Medinah Golf Club and got a free box of Life Savers with a hole in each one of them.

All of her guardians were single at the moment, though Budd had been married once, briefly. All, at times, had been college roommates of Gillian's father, Michael "Lefty" Saunders. But he had died in an accident one stormy night when he was driving home from a Big Ten football game, and Jojo, Budd, and Cory had suddenly found themselves legal guardians. They'd tried hard to be responsible and most often they were. Still, there were bad times like this when you were about to be alone in Chicago with a tornado on the way.

Right now there were plenty of people on hand, scrambling all over themselves trying to get ready to leave. The hotel barber was here too. He was the only one who didn't seem to be in any kind of hurry. While he shaved Jojo, his eyes were examining every corner of the room and darting glances through each door as if he'd never been in this suite before. Which didn't make sense.

She decided he was the snoopiest hotel employee she'd ever seen. Then she walked up behind him, her sneakers silent on the thick carpet. "Hey, you been with the Goldcoast East long?" she asked. "Or are you new here?"

He jumped and nearly took a slice out of Jojo's chin. Jojo sat up and said, "Hey yourself, Gill. Don't talk to the pilot, girl!" He waved her to a chair, but she was too restless to sit down. Instead, she thrust her hands in her pockets and studied her sometime-father.

"Jojo, you ever going to get married?"

A soapy Jojo sat up again in the make-do barber chair, which was the desk chair with a pillow added. "Now what makes you ask a dumb question like that?" he demanded. Then his black eyes considered her thoughtfully. "You pro or con on the subject, Gill?"

She hunched her shoulders and said nothing, turning it over in her mind. She had never really known Budd's wife. Some of Jojo's girl friends, most of them, were great to be with, funny and friendly and really helpful, but Jojo alone was still better. "I guess I don't know," she admitted.

"Well, I don't either, so let's leave it at that."

She was suddenly tired of standing and flopped into the nearest armchair. Apparently no worries about Jojo getting married right away, but what about the others? Who could ever tell what Budd might do? Or Cory? But she could ask Cory in person, day after tomorrow!

The very thought gave her a shiver of excitement. This time, day after tomorrow, she'd be in London, England,

and Cory would be there, ready to show her the works—Westminster Abbey, the Tower, the palaces, all of it. He was the best of the three about historical places. He never got to standing on one foot and then the other and looking at his watch and asking wasn't it about time for lunch.

Budd was the best for art galleries—he knew more about most of them than the paid guides did. He also liked beaches. In season or out. When it was too cold to swim, he'd take walks or race with you at water's edge. He'd help hunt for shells and strange pieces of driftwood. Jojo, of course, was the one for games—baseball, football, almost any; he only drew the line at roller derbies and ice hockey. She had the best of three worlds and usually no complaints. No reasonable complaints.

But today was different! Tonight and tomorrow would be dreadfully lonely. She didn't even want to think about how all alone she would be. Her most comforting possession was a snapshot of the four roommates taken the year they'd all lived in what they called the Magpie's Nest. She carried it in her wallet so she could study it whenever she felt the need. Like now.

Here, in a long-ago autumn-bright day on the porch steps of a big old-fashioned clapboard house, stood Michael Saunders, young and happy-looking. And Cory, light-haired and hazel-eyed, making a silly face. And Budd, with dark hair and gray eyes, and a tan that he kept all year by following the sun. Towering over his friends, Jojo—black and beautiful and knowing it.

She bent forward, her nose almost touching the snapshot's glossy surface.

"What's that you're looking at?" a sly voice asked.

She was startled. The barber had crept up behind her in a free moment while Jojo was taking a phone call. "What's it to you?" she snapped, covering the wallet with her shirt. "Go on, buzz off!"

Jojo had finished his phone call and was beckoning the barber. "Let's get this over with!"

Gillian clenched her hands tightly so she wouldn't bite a fingernail as she might have last year, and gazed gloomily at the busy people all around her. The suite, she decided, was *teeming*. Teeming was a word she'd found lately, liked, and was fast wearing out, but it fitted this situation exactly. Jojo's secretary was here, and his road manager, and a man from a recording company. There was also a booking agent who wanted Jojo to go on tour, singing his own songs, perched on a stool Rod McKuen style. Two reporters and a photographer had been here and gone. And Jojo's road manager, who was always jumpy and thought he was supposed to be a bodyguard, had lost his temper at a woman reporter who wouldn't leave and thrown a whole bucket of ice cubes at the wall. The woman had left without argument.

So Gillian was alone with six men. Usually she liked it that way, but today nothing satisfied her. She reached for the phone and dialed without even looking at the numbers.

The barber watched her. His gaze slid from her busy fingers to his own, slapping lotion on Jojo's face. "Who's she calling?" he demanded, then realized he'd spoken out loud and blushed clear down to his skinny neck. "I mean—she's just a kid—using your phone—" he squeaked into silence as Jojo stared at him.

Gillian thought of saying, "I'm calling the manager to

15

ask why you keep looking at everything—as if you thought somebody lost a diamond ring in here."

He had his eyes on Jojo, but she knew he was straining to hear her conversation. Except that she wasn't talking at all. She was listening to a weather report.

The telephone voice was feminine, but it was a voice of doom today. There was a tornado watch until midnight, the weather lady said cheerfully, with gusts, high winds, damaging hail likely, have a pleasant day and thank you for calling.

Tomorrow come gusts, hail or hellfire, Gillian Babcock Saunders had to board a plane at O'Hare and fly to Heathrow Airport, England, all by herself. Well, in a manner of speaking, all by herself. There would be the synthetically cheerful crew talking one-way at you like the weather voice, and there would be instructions on how to inflate a life jacket or breathe into an oxygen mask if it fell in your face. And it *would* fall in your face the minute anything went wrong. Every stewardess told you that.

There would be plenty of strangers all around her but she had orders not to tell her life story to any of them. Last year she talked too much to everyone whether she knew them or not, but she was too old for that now.

The barber had finally finished and was putting his tools away—taking his own sweet time about it, she noted. Jojo would be leaving any minute now. "Just don't make me sit in first class tomorrow," she begged him.

"Look here, Little Sister, I can afford it and I don't intend to worry about it," he said, climbing out of the chair.

"I'd *rather* sit in tourist, Jojo! I'd have a better chance to be with kids my own age."

"That's the *last* thing you better do," he said. "Just don't mess around with teen-agers when one of us can't be with you."

"Which is most of the time," she muttered, but Jojo heard.

He rolled his eyes heavenward and put out his hands, palms up, pleading. "You tuned in today, Lefty? You see what we have to contend with? Even Budd and Cory can't keep a jump ahead of her lately."

Gillian wasn't amused. "Budd and Cory haven't been *near* me lately!"

"They got to go where the job takes them, right? Same as I do."

"You don't even *like* movies—not your own anyway," she said accusingly. "You won't even watch yourself on T.V." But he was leaving her in dangerous weather to go finish a dumb movie he'd hate. Where was justice in this world?

"I like the paychecks," he said, "and I need them for the likes of you." He frowned at her steadily, deep in his own thoughts. "Look—do you think Budd could park himself in some Chicago office and still do his job? You think he'd find all those foreign authors in the Loop?"

"Well, I don't know why Cory wouldn't wait just a week for me. We could've sat together."

"I don't know why either," Jojo pretended to agree while his eyes mocked her. "I don't know why golfers always want to start their tournaments on schedule. Maybe this once they should've held the British Open in Lincoln Park so one spoiled rotten girl could have her favorite sportswriter handy. Right, sis?"

"Sis" usually meant that Jordan James was fed up, right up to the expensive Hollywood caps on his front teeth. She knew she was wrong. Those flaky heroines in romantic novels who were always wishing for a hole to crawl into and die maybe had a point, she decided.

But the Goldcoast East hadn't provided any holes for dying in. That was about the only item they'd skimped on. There were free flowers and baskets of fruit, free peanuts and free soft drinks in the refrigerator. The chairs were soft and the carpet was as deep as summer grass. For super-safety, at Jojo's request, the hotel had installed a chain and extra locks, and a peephole that swirled open and gave you a tiny look at whoever came to the door.

That reminded her—nobody would be coming to the door now. Everyone, including Jojo, would be leaving. And Gillian Babcock Saunders would have this fancy suite all to her lonesome self.

Jojo's road manager was warning him that if they didn't leave at once not even a tornado could get them to the airport on time. But Jojo remained standing solidly, hands on hips, studying Gillian. "I do not understand," he said, "how *any* girl wouldn't be glad to see Europe. 'Specially with her whole family taking turns to fetch and carry for her, tote her around first class, and show her the sights!"

When he started talking phony Southern-sounding, the danger point had been reached and passed. Even so she couldn't back down. She drew in a ragged breath and said, "Any toting you do will call for a mighty long reach, Jordan James. With me in London, England, and you in California, U.S.A.!"

"I'll be in the United Kingdom week after next," he told

her flatly. "I expect to be there before Cory has to leave. But he'll deliver you personally to Budd in Paris and I'll fetch you home. Any more complaints?"

Her stomach hurt. Not enough to get her hopes up, though. At camp a girl had gotten appendicitis and all kinds of attention.

Her folks had rushed upstate and stayed at her bedside but the girl had still griped about missing Parents' Day. And all because she wouldn't see Jojo, movie star and Black Comet.

It had been a wonderful day. Jojo had sung and played his guitar for the campers, parents, and counselors, and even for a lot of villagers from the closest town who either were movie fans or remembered old No. 23. It had been one of the proudest times of her life, Gillian decided in retrospect, but it was gone and Jojo would be, too, any minute.

Though she bent over and hugged both skinny forearms to her middle and groaned, no one listened. The barber had finally closed his equipment case but he wasn't leaving. He was moving sideways toward Jojo's bedroom, and Jojo was hollering, "Just where the devil do you think you're going?"

# 2

"Can't a guy even get a drink of water?" the barber whined.

Jojo shrugged and waved him on. Jojo had other things on his mind, but Gillian, watching the barber, thought, *he wants to snoop*. It didn't matter, though; all of Jojo's belongings were packed by now. Let the sneak help himself to an old tube of toothpaste if he wanted a souvenir. Everywhere Jojo went these days somebody tried to get his autograph or a piece of his necktie or even his shirttail if they could grab it.

Jojo said, "Listen, Gill, you'd better try smiling. You'll forget how." He rumpled her hair. "Didn't we find you a pretty good school? And a camp that wasn't too bad? Is it anybody's fault we all had to be somewhere else this week? Did we plan it that way?"

"I guess not." She hunched her shoulders and thrust her fists back in her pockets. Jojo hadn't any idea how it was to be even halfway scared. He hadn't been nervous at the Rose Bowl, nor with the Chicago Bears. You could bet on it. So how could she admit that she was terribly, terribly uneasy about flying to England all by herself? Shut up in a plane for seven hours!

"Well, how about a change of subject," Jojo suggested as if suddenly he had all the time in the world.

"Well, I saw one of your movies last night on T.V."

"Not that subject!" he said instantly.

"It was the one where some gamblers tried to get you to throw the big game."

"And pay off the mortgage on my mammy's piny woods cabin!"

Actually Jojo's mother lived in her own condominium in Acapulco and Gillian was always welcome there. It was a good thing to remember. It made her feel better.

"Call some bellboys," Jojo told his secretary. "Now look, Gill, take care. Watch the tube or read some of your books. Hey!"—he smacked his palms together as if coming out of a football huddle—"that reminds me, I got a book for Cory."

He told his secretary to fetch him a box out of the desk drawer in the bedroom. "You can take it to Cory, Gill. It won't take up much room."

The barber was being escorted to the door by Jojo's secretary, once a defensive end for the San Francisco '49ers. Jojo ignored them both and told Gillian he'd had a funny run-in about the box only this morning. "It's got somebody's old diary in it, I think. Bunch of handwritten stuff—some papers and a book. Cory likes that antique kind of jazz."

"Somebody's old diary?" she repeated. "If it's *really* old, I guess he'd read it. He wouldn't read my diary or yours, but if it was, I mean, were Napoleon Bonaparte's or somebody like that he'd like it."

Then she asked, "Did you get a present for Budd too?"

Or me? is really what she had in mind, and hoped Jojo understood. Actually she had nothing to complain about. He'd paid plenty for her trip. This wayward afternoon, though, she still felt terribly neglected and he ought to know it.

One of her faculty advisers at school had declared that Gillian Babcock Saunders was the absolute limit the way she often tried to play off her guardians against one another to get her own way and maximum attention. "Don't you think that's childish?" he'd asked.

"Maybe," she'd admitted, "but sometimes it works." And sometimes it helped to make up for what she'd never have in this world. A mother, who hadn't lived through the night Gillian was born. A real father. One place in the world to call home.

Jojo seemed to know where her thoughts were, but all he said was, "I didn't exactly go out and buy Cory a gift. It just sort of happened. Besides it's nothing to shout about."

His manager came back from the bedroom looking as if he smelled something he didn't like and handed her a tattered and dusty cardboard box. It must have been at least a hundred years old, she thought, and probably hadn't been much to start with. She made a face that must have matched the manager's and Jojo laughed.

"You see for yourself it's not exactly the Crown Jewels but some joker sure acted like it might be, this morning. Listen, honey, you take it to Cory and don't give it to anybody else. Cory will know what to make of it."

She put the box gingerly on the table by the telephone and wiped her fingers on the seat of her jeans. Jojo explained how he'd shopped again at the antique store where he'd bought Gillian a pin that used to belong to Mary Lincoln. "Remember that place, Gill?"

She nodded. Going antique-hunting with Jojo had been one of the best days of her life. He'd bought a stained-glass window about twelve feet high and had it shipped to his new house in California, and he'd bought about ten dozen other things including a 1914 calendar, an 1811 English reading glass, an ugly pug-dog iron doorstop, and a brooch that had papers to prove it once belonged to Mary Lincoln.

The store owner was a queer old fellow who probably hadn't taken inventory since 1899, Jojo said, and by now had accumulated more stuff than the city dump. But he was honest, no matter how absentminded and forgetful. It was one of Jojo's favorite shops and most of the furnishings in the game room of his new house had come from there.

"I wish I'd known you were going shopping today," Gillian sulked, "I could have gone too."

"Just as well you didn't. I got in a fight with a guy. I bought myself a tea can and this old box was lying inside. So I bought the whole works. I figured Cory would like the old papers."

"Tee can?" she asked. "A can to keep your tees in?"

"T-e-a can. A decorated tin deal that storekeepers used to have on the counter. Anyway another customer said this old box in the tea can was his—he'd just happened to drop it there while he was browsing. If he'd been halfway polite I might've let him have it. The box, I mean. I let him *have* it, all right, but not the way he wanted it."

Gillian blinked. "You mean you hit him? In that store

24

with all those Tiffany lamps, and dishes you can just about *see* through?"

"In the alley *next* to the store. I was taking a short cut home and this character tried to take *me* from behind. It didn't work."

He shooed the secretary and the others into the hall. She tried to think of something to say to keep him here even a minute longer. "It's so dirty!" she said. "It'll ruin all my new clothes!"

"Didn't I buy you a carry-on satchel just for your books?"

She nodded. Jojo had bought her a matched set of Louis Vuitton luggage, which she absolutely loved because she'd read about it in novels. French spies always carried it. Even George C. Scott had used it. In the movie where he was a hired gunman making his last run across Spain, he had opened the trunk of his car at a border crossing and displayed a suitcase exactly like one of hers.

Gillian also had a little trunk to be shipped all the way to Paris, bypassing London, and the satchel to slide under the plane seat. Her handbag could also be an over-the-shoulder bag. It looked like a feedbag and was open at the top so you could dump things in easily and get them out with no bother about zippers or snap locks. Jojo had tried to talk her out of it, warning that the International Society of Pickpockets would give it the best-design-of-the-year award. "But nobody wants anything a teen-ager is carry-ing," she'd said, victorious.

"Well, what about that satchel?"

"It's full of books. The one I bought for Cory and three books about Mary Lincoln—"

"Make it two books about Mary Lincoln and add that old box." Jojo sighed. "Doc will pick you up in plenty of time, which is more than I got. Be cool, Gill," he said, and was gone.

And Gillian was alone. It was so quiet all of a sudden that she could hear the air conditioner hum and the refrigerator purr in the little service kitchen.

Then thunder cracked. And rolled and muttered and died. She leaped for the radio and turned up the volume. It was playing "My Blue Heaven." That same tune had been playing off and on all week, and Jojo had told her it was an old, old song. "Before my time, even," he'd said.

"Do you think my mother used to dance to 'My Blue Heaven?'" she asked. But Jojo gave her a look and said, "I wouldn't be surprised if Mary Lincoln danced to it. Don't any of those books say?" He'd tapped the pile of biographies she'd collected.

She was reading a lot about Mary Lincoln these days. Partly because her class had been studying the Civil War last spring and she had chosen Mary Lincoln as the famous person to write about for her term paper. She had Mrs. Lincoln's brooch, thanks to Jojo, and that made the Lincolns and their times seem a little closer. She wanted to read more about them.

Now, abruptly, the suite vibrated with sounds. In the same instant the radio blared, thunder exploded, and the telephone rang. It was the hotel operator. Paris, France, was calling the Jordan James suite.

"Is Mr. James in?"

"No," Gillian said, "but I am. It's my Uncle Budd. He

26

calls me all the time." He didn't, but whose business was that?

Budd spoke over the line clearly but in French, probably to see if she'd kept up her lessons. She hadn't, so he switched to American with only dashes of Italian and Spanish.

"Where's Jojo, *querida?* I've got great news for both of you—you'll never guess what!"

"Yes, I can!" she yelled into the phone, with tears suddenly smarting her eyes. "Oh, Budd, you can't! You just *can't!* Not this summer!" She remembered the voice and words all too vividly from the past—Budd saying, "I've got great news—you'll never guess what!"

"Do you have any idea what we're talking about?" he asked after a tiny pause.

"You're getting married again!"

"Did I say that?"

"You didn't have to—you said 'great news'—that's what you said before. I remember." There was a longer pause and it made her nervous. "Well, is she French or what?"

"Put Jojo on," Budd said flatly.

"I can't. He's in Doc Sawyer's limousine. They've gone to O'Hare. He's going back to California and there's a tornado coming."

Budd said something in French or Italian that sounded like swearing. "What about your trip—is that off?"

"I'm coming to England by myself," she said, trying not to whine. "And I guess Cory will bring me to Paris."

"That's what I'm calling about," Budd said. "I won't *be* in Paris. I've bought a house in Italy. You and Cory fly to

27

Pisa; I'll meet you there. Wire me arrival time. Can you write this down? I'll be in Camaiore." He spelled it for her. "I won't have a phone—"

Somebody was leaning on the door buzzer. She yelled, "Wait a minute!" And to Budd, "There's someone in the hall—can you hang on till I answer?"

"No!" Budd yelled. "Not at these prices. Listen, Gill, I'll try to get in touch with Cory and give him directions. *Ciao, tesoro.*" "Good-by, treasure," Gillian translated and smiled.

Budd had hung up but the buzzer hadn't quit. She ran across to use the peephole the way Jojo had told her. Maybe the storm had grounded him and he was too much in a hurry to use their signal, beep-beep-de-beep!

But it wasn't her guardian waiting at the door. It was the barber. He was looking both ways up and down the corridor and rubbing his palms together.

"What is it?" she asked through the peephole.

"Let me in there, kid. I left my clippers and I ain't got all day."

She hesitated while he glared at the door as if he could see in. "The way I got shoved out of there it's a wonder I didn't leave the whole works. Let me in, miss."

"I'll go look," she said. She wasn't about to let him in, even if he weren't a total stranger. Jojo had rules about strangers and Gillian had her own rule about people she didn't like.

She glanced over the tables and the floor, and the chair that had been used as a barber stool. Then she looked in Jojo's bathroom just to be sure the dummy hadn't carried them in there.

"No clippers," she reported back.

"Let me in, kid. They could've dropped behind somethin'. I *got* to get them back—they ain't even mine!"

Wheedling wouldn't do it. Gillian Babcock Saunders knew all about wheedlers. "I'll call the manager," she said, "and let *him* look, okay?"

"Now hold on! Listen, I'll tell the maid—she can find 'em. You're going to let the maid in, aren't you?" He sneered at the peephole. "Anyway I'm leaving, so don't bother nobody, hear?"

"I don't think you lost any clippers!" she called after him, perversely. "Just buzz off!"

Then she went to the window to see if the storm had gone away too. It hadn't.

# 3

There were free fireworks over Lake Michigan. Black waves rolled and turned crazy somersaults while the beaches lay stark and still. Along Outer Drive traffic crawled in a blur of lights.

She looked at her watch, a super watch Budd had once brought from Switzerland. Six o'clock Daylight Saving Time in storm-darkened Chicago. Suppertime, but she wasn't hungry. That was a help. She wouldn't have to deal with any waiters or open the door, or figure out a tip, or anything.

She could even go to bed. Who was to know or care if a person decided she might feel more comfortable in bed early on a tornado-watch night?

All through lunchtime Jojo had been working on one of his poems. He said anybody could write poetry, but that was open to doubt. He'd won the Paul Laurence Dunbar Poetry Award in college, and his friend Gwendolyn Brooks, a Pulitzer Prize winner and Poetess Laureate of Illinois, said his poems had bones and muscle, and to forget about Dunbar or any other poet and just write what he had to say.

Anyway he'd forgotten to order lunch until it was nearly three o'clock and then he'd had a whole banquet brought in. So Gillian wasn't hungry. Not even for a milk-shake or a hamburger. And she didn't feel like watching television.

She wasn't dirty or sleepy either, but she took a hot shower and got into her pajamas and climbed into bed. At least she had a brand-new book called *Mary Lincoln, One of Ours*. It might keep her mind off storms and to-morrows, and it might make her sleepy.

All it did, though, was make her wider awake and ready to argue. She wished Cory were here right now, not just to travel with her tomorrow afternoon, but to talk about this book.

Mary Lincoln, a women's liberator? The author of *Mary Lincoln, One of Ours* was someone Gillian had never heard of. She had a pinchy-looking mouth in the back cover photograph, and no eyelashes, and she was wearing a baseball cap.

She was trying to prove that Mrs. Lincoln had tried to free the women of her day just as her husband had tried to free the slaves. Mrs. Lincoln's habit of running up big bills for clothes was one way of getting back at her husband and the "male-dominated" household and staff.

Mrs. Lincoln had point-lace shawls, cashmere shawls, paisley shawls, opera cloaks, and a feather cape—the author was right about that, Gillian had read it in other books. But she had always thought Mary Lincoln was just trying to keep warm in drafty rooms with only little potbellied stoves or fireplaces for heat.

In any case, having shawls and brooches and gold brace-lets and a lace parasol cover wasn't Gillian's idea of strik-ing out at anything in particular. Southern ladies before the war were always dressed up in hoop skirts and flounces, velvets and braids and laces from France, and brooches made of real hair. Brooches! The word leaped into her mind and she started out of bed almost simultaneously.

Her bag was packed but it wasn't closed. Suppose that sneaky barber had got in here when nobody was paying attention? He'd been after something, she was sure of it.

But Mary Lincoln's pretty pin was still safe in the satin case with the rest of Gillian's valuables: a wristwatch that didn't run but had belonged to her father; a gold locket that had her mother's baby picture in it and had belonged to her grandmother, an ivory letter opener with little elephants walking along its topside which one of Budd's Korean authors had given to her for luck, and a medal Jojo had won at a track meet in high school.

Everything was still safely in place. She went back to bed and picked up the book and tried to forget her worries.

The author's main argument seemed to be that Mary Lincoln had taken fifty or sixty cartons along with half a dozen or so trunks when she had to leave Washington for good. This had stirred up Congress and the newspapers, whether or not it was any of their business. The author said the whole country was "hostility-oriented" against the widow and clamoring to know what was in those boxes and trunks. But nobody had found out for certain. And what did it matter now? It was all so long ago. Mrs. Lincoln had problems enough in her own day—she didn't need this author in a baseball cap bringing up new arguments.

Gillian pulled her knees up to her chin and sat hunched in the frilly bed in the prettiest, or meant to be, room of

the suite. The bed was regal, she decided; the whole room was regal—powder-blue and damask-looking, with antique-white, wobbly-legged furniture. Maybe Marie Antoinette would have put her stamp of approval on this room but Gillian thought it was frothy and useless. It didn't keep the lightning flashes away.

They were, in fact, getting worse, so she counted to twenty in Spanish and to eight in French and to three in Italian, which was the most she could manage at the moment. She took her time about it, just to show the storm she was still in control here. Then she bolted out of bed and ran to Jojo's room and climbed between the fresh, cool and crisp, green sheets.

There wasn't a trace of Jojo here. Not even a few lines of the poetry he'd been working on this afternoon. The tables looked like parade drums and the chairs and bed were covered in a quilted red, green, and gold plaid. British guardsmen in framed lithographs stood at attention on the wall. No frills and no satin here. It was a sensible room, but lonely.

She punched her head hard into both pillows. The night still thundered and her stomach hurt; so she went into the bathroom and threw two of the fluffy unused towels into the tub and tore the cellophane off the drinking glasses and decided it looked more as if somebody lived here.

Back in bed she decided to count sheep, which was silly and childish, but maybe it would work. It didn't. She was at the count of ninety-nine when the doorbell buzzed again.

If that barber was back she would call the manager. Jojo had said she could call in any case of real worry. "But not if a window shade flaps," he'd added.

Well then, she would scare the barber by just threatening the call. No big deal. She slid out of bed and padded across the thick emerald green carpeting in her bare feet.

"What do you want *this* time?" she yelled, even before she looked through the peephole. But it wasn't the barber. It was a waiter.

"Room service, *señorita*," he said.

"I didn't order anything," Gillian said.

"It's your supper, *señorita*."

He was thin and patient. He kept his eyes lowered, held the covered tray with one hand, and waited.

She studied him through the peephole and wondered if maybe Jojo *had* left instructions for sandwiches or a bedtime snack to be brought up.

"What did he order?" she asked.

"Your supper, *señorita*."

"What's on the tray I mean?"

"I doan know," he shrugged, eyes still lowered. Did he know she was watching him?

"Well, I guess it's all right," she started to say, but before the words were out the elevator doors opened down the corridor out of her sight but not out of the waiter's. He looked startled and moved a little closer to the door as if to hide himself, tray and all.

Whoever came out of the elevator went down the hall the other way and the waiter stood up straighter and looked stiffer than a cardboard cutout.

"I don't want it—thanks very much, *muchas gracias!*" She wished he didn't look so dogged and patient as if he might wait there forever until she opened the door.

"Take it back. *Pronto*, okay?"

"You going to get me in trouble, *señorita*. What I going to do with it?"

"Eat it. Take it home. I don't care and I won't tell anybody. There's no one here anyway—" then she covered her mouth with her hand. Now that was a dumb thing to admit. "No one yet, I mean. So hurry up, make tracks."

She went back to her chair and curled up as tight as possible. Nerves were childish. It was just her imagination working overtime to think that the waiter was still standing out there. He couldn't get in because Jojo had insisted on that chain lock besides the regular locks which the maids and the bellboys could open when they needed to.

Jojo used this suite whenever he was in Chicago and he was the kind of tipper who usually got his own way. Jojo had grown up in parts of this town where extra locks were a way of life. He wasn't going to take unnecessary chances.

So she was perfectly safe from strangers here unless she decided to open the door, and she wasn't about to do that, so why be jumpy? She had her tickets and her passport, her certificate of vaccination, whether she needed it or not, and spending money, and even a cellophane bag with twenty dollars' worth of British money in it.

And tomorrow Doc would call for her in plenty of time to get to O'Hare. Doc ran his limousine service for all kinds of important people. He hauled movie people and rock stars and politicians and star athletes all the time. He had been a football player in Jojo's day and they were good friends. No worries about getting to the airport—she just wished Doc could drive her to London.

She wasn't worried about a hijacking or an accident. It

37

was what Budd called the closed-in jumps that bothered her. He sometimes had a case of them himself, or so he claimed. He said you'd never catch him visiting Mammoth Cave or Carlsbad Caverns no matter how many millions of tourists did.

The trip tomorrow would be seven hours and six or seven minutes. A long time to feel like a sardine, canned, but still alive. A big plane was just a bigger can with more sardines.

Thunder boomed closer now, and she said aloud, "Hey, Dad, I'm not going to be scared, I promise." And trembled as the door buzzer hummed furiously for the third time.

# 4

A maid stood in the hall pressing the buzzer with steady concentration. There were towels over her forearm. Perspiration glistened on her low, wide forehead. She looked as angry as the door buzzer sounded.

"I don't need anything," Gillian told her, keeping an eye at the peephole. This was not the regular maid on the evening shift. Mary Kelly *her* name was, and she had told Gillian how much she wished she could go with her—if there could be a way to float down nice and easy into Ireland as the plane passed over Shannon.

"I don't need any towels," Gillian said again, to the strange and fierce-looking maid. "Thank you anyway."

Maids had their days off same as anybody but tonight of all nights Gillian wished Mary Kelly were here. This maid was twice as big as Mary and she had a downy mustache.

Her feet were planted wide apart and her beady little eyes had a glint that warned, "Don't give me any trouble." Gillian had read about beady little eyes but up till this minute she'd thought only stuffed animals and rag dolls actually had hard shiny eyes.

"Will you kindly open that door, miss? I have to turn down the bed."

"They're turned down," Gillian was happy to say honestly. "I've already been in both of them."

The woman set her thin lips even more tightly and took some keys from her pocket. But thanks to Jojo's wisdom the door wouldn't open more than a couple of inches.

"You'll have to release the chain, young lady!"

"Where's Mary Kelly?" Gillian asked, not budging.

The woman's forehead wrinkled in thought. "She took sick." Then she put on a pasty grin that somehow was even more frightening than her scowl. "She'll be back tomorrow, Little Missie."

That's right! Gillian thought. She remembered now: Mary Kelly was going to a family party tonight honoring a much-loved uncle's first visit to America. Mary had talked about it all week.

"How sick is she?" Gillian asked slyly. "Was her illness sudden, would you say?" *Why* was this terrible looking woman lying to her? What was the matter with everybody tonight?

"It's nothing to worry about," the maid said. "She just come down with a sinus headache about an hour ago and she hadda ask me to take over this floor along with my own. I got plenty to do, miss, how long do you intend to keep me standing out here?"

"You can leave anytime, ma'am," Gillian said. "I already told you—I don't need a single thing. Thank you kindly, ma'am."

*Make tracks!* she yearned to shout. *You awful person, pretending Mary Kelly is sick! What do you want in this room?* Then she remembered, and the pounding of her heart eased. "There aren't any clippers in here—I already looked."

"Listen, miss, I got to turn down those beds. That's my job. You want to get me fired?"

"Oh my good golly, no!" she yelled. "I don't want to bother anybody! I don't want anybody to bother me! Just go away—please!"

She ran on tiptoe across the room feeling pursued, afraid to look behind her. She threw herself into the armchair and glared into the half darkness. Maybe the storm had gotten on everybody's nerves. Why had this big scary maid lied? Why had the barber pretended to lose his clippers? *Clippers!* She sat up. He hadn't even *used* clippers. He'd only shaved Jojo, hadn't trimmed his hair, nor been asked to. And that waiter had brought a meal she'd never ordered . . .

The phone was right beside her. Waiting. Ready for a call for help. But what could she say? I don't like the maid's mustache? *Don't get flaky, Gillian,* she told herself silently but firmly. And sighed.

Her eyes roamed the gloom seeking comfort. The dirty old box that Jojo wanted Cory to have was still on the table where she'd left it. She'd better pack it now while she thought about it.

It was just as shabby and disreputable-looking as ever. She didn't want to try hiding it under her new clothes unless she could find a wrapping for it. She didn't even want it to rub off on the covers of the new books in her carry-on bag. She combed the suite looking for something suitable but there wasn't anything that would do for wrapping paper.

The bureau drawers and desk drawers had pretty stick-down linings, not loose paper. There was stationery in the desk but all that was left was airmail and it was too small and flimsy.

If she had tape, she could use the stationery and make a fairly neat package, but there wasn't any tape in the desk. She tried the kitchen again. Jojo's manager, who was always nibbling, had left behind a package of cheese, some crackers, half a bottle of dry-roasted nuts, and a box of Mrs. Burton's home-style butter cookies, untouched. No paper and no tape, but she studied the cookie box. It looked to be just the right size for Cory's gift to fit inside. If she could open the carton without tearing the cellophane she could reseal it and who would ever know the difference?

She was wary when it came to customs. Not to be caught hiding anything was very, very important. She'd had one terrible experience coming back from Mexico with Budd and she'd solemnly vowed there'd never be another like it. Gillian Babcock Saunders was never going to embarrass anyone at a customs counter ever again.

The Mexico experience had also taught her that gifts for people can be treacherous too. Sometimes anyway. Like this tacky old box. Who would believe it was a present for Cory if you didn't know that he liked antique things? Customs men were quick and thorough and they didn't care about your feelings when they searched your luggage.

The Mexican fiasco, as Budd called it, had all started on a beach at Puerto Vallarta. She discovered you could just be sitting in the sun minding your own business and about ten dozen people, even kids and really old people, would come up and try to sell you things. They were walking department stores. With live snakes, art works, ceramics, fried fish on a stick, hats, bags, trays, and dishes painted while you waited.

Dozens of boys Gillian's age had trudged back and forth all day in their bare feet, floppy hats, white shirts, and white pants. They were friendly but so convinced that you would buy something because you were a *turista* you were lucky not to be buried under purchases. She'd bought a big woven sombrero for Budd, which she could tell he didn't really want.

Then Budd was summoned back to the hotel to take a business call and disaster had struck in his absence, though she hadn't realized it at the time. She'd been offered a girdle at a great bargain, or so the salesman claimed. It was a black lacy affair with two red, red hearts appliquéd on it. No matter that she was just past her twelfth birthday then and needed a girdle about as much as a snake did. The Mexican had a nice smile and she bought the garment.

Before Budd came back, she had second thoughts about the purchase and hid it in her beach bag. However, it had not stayed hidden. The customs man in Chicago had dived for it and held it up for the world to view, including Budd's maybe-to-be second wife, who was watching through the glass windows upstairs at the International arrivals section of O'Hare Airport.

"Which a' you belongs to this?" the customs clown had asked, and the red hearts had seemed twice, ten times, as scarlet as they had on a sun-bright beach. But by no means as red as Budd's handsome face. No matter how deep his tan was or how supercool he acted, Budd proved he could blush like anybody else.

But the man had kept right on waving her purchase for

what seemed an eternity. It turned out that he knew Budd well because Budd was practically a commuter to and from Europe and seldom carried anything interesting, only duty-free gifts well under his allowance, and this terrible man was just having a bit of fun on a dull day. Budd had sworn he'd never take Gillian so far as Gary, Indiana, again. Not for six or seven years, he'd said. But later he'd reduced the sentence to one year with good behavior because he didn't want to marry the girl who'd been upstairs that day after all and Gillian's girdle had helped him make up his mind.

For the wife-to-be hadn't thought the red hearts were funny and was worried someone would think the girdle had been meant for her. And she hadn't thought "dragging somebody else's brat around all the time" was a picnic either. Gillian had overheard her saying so and felt both furious and guilty about it.

"I don't think it's fair for you to criticize her about the customs thing," Gillian told Budd, still guilty but relieved. "You didn't think it was funny either."

"I do now," he'd said. "Okay?"

So maybe that disaster had worked out for the best, but Gillian Saunders was going to be leery of customs from now on. And so took plenty of time to open the cookie box. She didn't care if it took all night. It didn't though; the wrappings opened easily. She put the cookies on a plate in the refrigerator in case Mary Kelly or the day maid would want them.

And in their place went the box. Mrs. Burton had been thoughtful enough to pack her material in heavy aluminum

foil, and it was no trick to crimp it back into place like new.

Then Gillian carefully heated the cellophane outside wrapping with her traveling iron and the tricky stuff made the same folds and magically stuck like cement. She would bet that nobody this side of Scotland Yard would suspect the box had ever been opened.

Mrs. Burton's home-style butter cookies went into Gillian's carry-on satchel with the books, and Gillian went back to bed in the British guardsmen's room. It wasn't just because Jojo had sat at the desk and worked there this afternoon. Not at all. Green was her favorite color. And the lightning hadn't found this room. Even the thunder seemed farther away.

She stared at the ceiling and thought about giving the weather lady one last buzz for old times sake but decided against it, in case of more bad news. She worried a little about whether it was legal to take butter cookies into the United Kingdom, but decided it was.

She was not going to sleep tonight. That was for sure. But she closed her eyes, just for a moment, and was surprised when she opened them to a roomful of daylight.

The telephone was ringing, and the door buzzer was sounding just as steady and non-stop as it had last night when the maid brought the towels.

# 5

In the cluttered back room of a gaunt, dingy, ready-to-be-condemned building in Chicago's Old Town, two men talked. That is, one of them talked and the other mostly scratched his ear and listened.

The man who scratched was the barber from the Gold-coast East hotel. He was jumpier and more fretful than ever. The other was T. D. Mattson, co-owner of the Roudy Goudy bookstore, which was housed in the front part of the ramshackle building.

Mattson and his partner, Kurt Durkin, sold out-of-print books and art works, and occasionally had a few other irons in the fire. Mattson himself had been well into the fire more than once, but was cool at the moment. He still sold the same kind of books and prints that had once got him a jail sentence but now nobody seemed to care. At least not on Wells Street.

His other jail sentence, in a pinch and scramble past, involved a case of literary forgery. He'd met his partner, Durkin, during this period behind bars. Durkin had been serving time for a criminal act that had nothing to do with books. Mattson, though, had once been a dedicated and even brilliant dealer in rare books and manuscripts, a true

47

scholar of Americana, but luck ran against him and he'd gone broke being honest.

Bankruptcy and a poverty-nurtured envy of success had led Mattson to the low but profitable art of forgery.

He'd often read about and rather admired the greatest scoundrels in the field of deceit: hoaxes for pay, forgery of documents and letters. He was sure that his own scholarship in the field would aid him in becoming a master of the craft. He would choose his area very carefully.

He decided, therefore, to limit his forgeries strictly to American authors and historical personages of the eighteenth and nineteenth centuries, which was the kind of inverse patriotism duped customers later complained about. One of his best "subcontractors," however, had been a whiz at reproducing Benjamin Franklin's handscript and signature, and in several ventures a good deal of money had been pocketed—though largely by the subcontractor.

But cleverness was eclipsed by greed, and greed led to downfall. This same wretch had penned a letter supposedly written by Nathan Hale early in October of 1776 to his bootmaker, complaining about a loose sole that hurt his foot. The letter was a gem of discontent such as any sensitive gentleman might compose. The Hale signature was nearly flawless, enough so to pass all tests.

But what Mattson and his pen man forgot, as the intended buyer did *not*, was that Nathan Hale's feet weren't hurting in October. General George Washington's volunteer spy had been executed by the British on the morning of September 22, 1776.

T. D. Mattson and the forger each lost a year and a half of freedom for that error, and Mattson became acquainted with Kurt Durkin, another bookish prisoner. Now the partnership was about to launch a new endeavor toward riches and fame. Not in forgery, however; this time Mattson was sure he had his hands on the real thing.

Or *did* have until it got away. For he had lost it in the most unbelievable mix-up imaginable. Now he would have to share its recovery with his partner, Kurt Durkin, whom he hated and envied more than anyone else in the world. Durkin was a psychopath, and a clever one: ruthless, avaricious, tenacious, and able to change colors like a chameleon, squirming into situations and even social circles where he could most harm others while helping himself. Mattson would have given anything to have pulled off this job without Durkin's knowledge. But now he had to rely on him. And on the small army of thugs he'd deployed to investigate anybody who came near the box.

At the moment Durkin was on the West Coast, making certain Jordan James hadn't taken the treasure with him while pretending to send it to England with the kid. While T.D. was in Chicago chastizing his brother-in-law. "I told you to get in there and find out where he put that box! Just to *find out*, that's all!"

"I *did* get in, T.D. I paid off the guy who was s'posed to go. I *got* in! I couldn't see nothin' then he told one of his creeps to give it to the kid. I hung aroun' as long as I could. Even went to the bathroom. Hellsfire, you shoulda seen! Half them guys are football players. And that kid! She's got eyes like a' alley cat." T.D. sighed heavily. His head still throbbed from the bump he'd gotten when James had flung him against the antique-store wall yesterday morning. He decided to try patience, spell-it-all-out patience, so that maybe this idiot would remember something important.

"Look at me," he said. "Do I look like a football player? Am I going to hurt you?"

"No," the barber said cautiously.

"I am not a football player," T.D. said very evenly, clenching his teeth between words. "I am a highly educated, cultured man. A quiet, gentle man. A *business* man. I have a reputation to maintain. I told you this box belongs to me. I just left it in that tea can while I was looking at some other things. Trying to make up my mind about other things—" He had left it in the tea can, which to his certain knowledge had sat there unsold for at least five years and gone off to feign interest in a Tiffany lamp. He had planned then to glance at the tea can—just by chance—and buy it quickly, with the box safely inside and riding free. Except that the big, black, ignorant football player had hustled him.

There was some comfort in knowing it hadn't been merely cheapness that led him to hide the box inside the tea can instead of buying it outright. The store owner knew him well. The old fox would want to look very, very carefully at any book Mattson or Durkin would buy. Chances were he wouldn't sell either one of them a book. A tea can, sure, but no books, letters, or manuscripts. The tea can had been around unsold for years. How could anybody figure that jigaboo would come along and slap down twenty bucks for it?

But *even then*, Mattson remembered in real agony, if he hadn't lost his head he could have gotten the box back. But he'd followed James out of the store and demanded it back. The jig had said, "You ever ask for anything politely, man?" And that's when Mattson had gone a little crazy and said, "Just hand it over, boy!"

A major mistake. The jig had told his driver to see that the can got shipped to the Coast and announced in Uncle-Tom talk, "I think I'll try to read me this book," and brushed Mattson aside and strolled off down the alley.

"You got a lump like a mushroom on your head, T.D.," his brother-in-law noted. T.D. also had a complexion like a mushroom and the same aversion to sunlight. He wore a handlebar mustache that drooped fashionably, but his long teeth protruded badly. And his black slicked-down hair looked as slippery as his character.

"Now try and tell me everything that happened," T.D. said, "from the beginning."

"I already did."

"Then tell me why, why, *Why*, you asked that spic waiter to try and get in?"

"The kid wouldn't let *me* in. She acted like I was a thief or something." The barber hunched his thin shoulders and dug at a bite on his neck. "The Mex was the only one I knew as broke as me, even worse. You said 'Don't scare the kid,' T.D., that's exactly what you said. Make it seem natural, don't force her to yell for help. I figured she'd be used to waiters coming and going—Anyway I done the best I could think of—"

He put his shaky hands together and rubbed the palms. He'd never been mixed up in anything like this before and he hoped—no, he *swore*, he'd never do anything for T.D. again. He'd never borrow another dime from his brother-in-law. He'd go on relief before he'd help T.D. even if it was only to find a crummy box that T.D. said was his property. "I took a big chance, T.D.," he said. "I ain't even a regular. I'd never of got on if it hadn't been so many guys were on vacation and one busted up in a car wreck."

He was sorry he'd brought the Mexican waiter into it. That maid was something else though. She'd been hired by Durkin and she was a holy terror. He hated to think what might have happened to the kid if the maid had got in.

As a matter of fact, the barber thought, he wouldn't put it past the maid to try again this morning. But he'd better not tell T.D. that. It might not fit in with T.D.'s plans. T.D. said Durkin had given orders *nobody* was to scare the kid.

"Incompetents!" T.D. again sighed heavily. "I should never have relied on amateurs. From now on Durkin and I will handle the job and you just keep your mouth shut."

"Can I go now, T. D.?"

"You can go," said T.D., "when you've told me *everything* that black boy said and did before they threw you out, and *everything* you heard in the hall. You *did* listen, didn't you?"

"I listened, T.D." He wished to God he hadn't. He was sure the kid had the box and he didn't like to think what they might do to her if she tried to get cute about it and maybe not hand it right over when Durkin caught up with her. Because Durkin wasn't right in the head.

# 6

She reached for the phone and at the same time called out, "hold on a minute!" to whoever was leaning on the door buzzer. But the unseen person kept on zinging.

"Hello!" she bellowed into the phone, forgetting to lower her voice.

"Ee-YOW" Jojo hollered back. Then his voice grew dim and distant. "Well, how's it going, Gill? Did I wake you up?"

"You, among others. Jojo, there's somebody at the door making a terrible racket. And you sound funny. What's the matter?"

"*Nada, niente,* nothing. Listen, Gill, *forget* the door and pay attention. There's something important I forgot to tell you—"

"Well, fine, but I could hear better if I answered the door first—"

"NO!" he shouted. "Don't answer it! Let it go, Gill. Stay right there and hang on just half a second—" Then the sound was muffled as if he had put his hand over the speaker and was talking to someone else. Jojo seldom counted how long you kept up a phone connection, even long distance, prime time. He'd let you put the phone down and go look up something you wanted to read to him. He'd even help with math problems. He was acting very peculiar this morning.

"Listen, Gill," he said, "you know that friend of yours—that buddy from school, Mary somebody?"

"Mary Agatha? You mean Mary Agatha Pierce, my roommate?" She sat up and kicked off the covers.

"That's the one!" He said it as if she'd answered a prize-winning stumper.

"She's a creep. What about her?" Mary Agatha wasn't really *too* creepy but it was still raining and Gillian felt gloomy.

"Well, her mother's not a creep," Jojo said impatiently.

"Mrs. Pierce is okay," she admitted. What on earth did Mrs. Pierce or Mary Agatha have to do with Jojo in Southern California? The Pierces lived in Highland Park, Illinois, about thirty or forty minutes north of where Gillian was this minute.

Mary Agatha was her best friend sometimes, sometimes not. They'd been roommates at school for two years, which was a lot of time to spend with a person who was practically perfect in everything she tried. Even at French verbs and ice skating, and the guitar. And she was always going out for something new. All this spring Mary Agatha had been a vegetarian and wouldn't wash her hair in real shampoo, just in some brew she had boiled up from vegetables. And Mary Ag had a mother and a father who were almost perfect, and a brother who wasn't half bad, plus about ten dozen best friends who all thought she was perfect too.

Mrs. Pierce played tennis and knitted sweaters for Mary

Ag and taught school—a Head Start program—in what Jojo said was a *really* underprivileged neck of the woods. She had to drive there five days a week in the winter, about sixty miles round trip, even though Mr. Pierce was an architect and they lived in a big beautiful house right out of a glossy magazine.

"Are you listening, California? Mrs. Pierce has a tennis elbow," Gillian announced over the phone. "This is your eight A.M. trivia broadcast live from beautiful rain-soaked Chicago glug glug—"

"Oh, knock it off, will you, Gill?" Jojo was brisk now. "Here's what I forgot to tell you in all the rush yesterday—Mary Agatha and her mother are going to pick you up this morning, in about half an hour in fact. They'll help you get it all together and get out of there. They've got some big plans—the Field Museum, I think—"

"The Field Museum?" she yelled. "On the day I got to fly to London, England?"

She was suddenly aware that the room was quiet.

"Hey, Jojo," she whispered, "he went away—whoever it was."

"Good," Jojo said. He took a deep breath you could hear clear across the country. "So you be ready when Mrs. Pierce phones from the lobby. She's on her way right this minute. You wait there till she calls and let her come up and help you with your stuff. Let her call the bellboy, hear?" He was speaking in a don't-get-excited, you-can-do-it tone.

"How do you know she's on her way?" Gillian asked, spacing her words too. "How can you tell from way out there?"

"Well, chances *are*," he said, after a pause. "She knows you haven't got all day."

All day was *exactly* what she had. She looked at her watch. She'd worn it to bed for comfort. It had a luminous dial and the hands kept moving very matter-of-factly, business as usual, no matter how strange everything else might seem in the night. Or lonely.

Last night's awful feeling in her stomach came back and started to creep upward, drying her throat so that she could hardly swallow. But at least the buzzing had stopped.

"Is it okay if I order breakfast?" she asked, "or did you order that too? Like supper."

"I didn't order supper," he said sharply, "but there ought to be some food in that kitchen, enough to hold you till lunch. You don't want to keep the Pierces waiting while you horse around with room service."

"All right," she agreed. "But I still can't believe Mary Ag wants to come downtown on a day like this and drag around in the rain and leave all her friends. They always got sixteen different things to do every single day!"

"Then it's extra nice of her to want to see you off," Jojo pointed out. "And just this once you might try to act halfway thankful, like a nice, grown-up girl, hear?"

"See me off?" she yelled. "What about Doc Sawyers? You told me Doc would pick me up!"

"Well, he planned to, but something came up. And the Pierces are really counting on seeing you right to the plane. How's that for service?"

The dryness in her throat was choking her. "What came up?" she demanded. "What's the matter with Doc?" It was a really rotten feeling not to be told anything. Especially today.

"He wrenched his back, is all."

"How?" she asked. "He was all right yesterday."

"At the airport." Jojo's voice was dim again as if he had backed off from the phone, or was thinking about something else. "He'll be all right. No big deal. Besides, Mrs. Pierce can help you pack. Doc wouldn't know how to do that."

"I'm packed! I even got the box in my carry-on bag."

"Say, that's right," Jojo said, in a just-happened-to-think-of-it way. She knew *that* tone. She'd heard it often enough. ("Hey, Gill, guess what, we found a private school you're going to like—" or "We've found this great new girl's camp—")

"Well, listen," Jojo said, "I don't know why we want to bother Cory with that old thing when he's busy at the golf tournament. You just give it to Mrs. Pierce and she can keep it for him. He can look it over when he gets back. Okay?"

Well, that was a relief! She'd be glad to leave it.

"Sure," she said. "Right-o!"

"So stay loose," Jojo was saying, "and I'll see you next week."

"Cheerio," she said. "Pip pip, *adieu!*"

The rain was a wet memory. Sunlight streamed through the windows and Gillian was flying to England today. Things could be a lot worse. She wondered if London would be as wonderful as it was in books and movies. Cory could be counted on to show her everything. Even the Old Curiosity Shop and Windsor Castle. He didn't care how many times he'd seen things like that. He enjoyed them and made you have the time of your life, wherever you were.

Gillian laid out her traveling clothes and hurried through her shower. She had just finished tying her sneakers when the phone rang again to announce the Pierces' arrival. Mary Ag would probably be comfortably clad in shorts and any old top. But Gillian Saunders had to wear something suitable for crossing an ocean. A salesgirl in a department store on Michigan Avenue had helped her decide on red denims, a candy-striped turtleneck and a navy sweater.

She took one quick last look in the carry-on bag before she zipped it shut: Mary Lincoln biographies, a "comfort bag" of candy bars, chewing gum, cheese crackers, and comic books. And Mrs. Burton's home-style butter cookies.

"If you get nervous," Jojo had said, "eat some candy or chew some gum."

Then he'd added, "Or crumple up those comics and stuff them in your mouth if you feel like yelling. Yells don't set well with other passengers."

By now the Pierces were buzzing at the door. She ran to open it, slamming back all the locks, feeling foolish in daylight because there were so many. Mary Ag was wearing jeans and a stretch top that was new, and new sneakers. Gillian liked the sneakers better than the top. Mary Ag had the same brown eyes, brown hair, and freckles she'd always had but her figure was getting curvier while Gillian's seemed to grow straighter and flatter. One of these days Gillian Babcock Saunders was going to have a heart-to-heart talk with Jojo and find out if her mother had been a string bean all her life. That was what a hateful kid at camp had called Gillian. It wasn't important. But she thought about it just the same.

Mrs. Pierce was as cheerful as ever and told Gillian how nice she looked and how practical, wearing pants for a long journey. Then she began to go quickly through closets and drawers and even the medicine chests in both bathrooms to be certain nothing of importance had been left behind.

It almost seemed as if Mrs. Pierce was hunting for something. But that was ridiculous.

Mary Ag said, "I'm glad I'm not you today. Boy, would I hate to go all that way by myself!"

"There'll be about three hundred people with me," Gillian said. "Do we *have* to go to the Field Museum?"

Mrs. Pierce came back into the living room and said, "No, now that the sun's out we can try the sidewalk art fair in Skokie—how does that sound to you?" But she didn't wait for an answer. She cast a puzzled glance around the room and finally asked, "Gillian, honey, isn't there something you want to leave with me? I believe your guardian—Mr. James—said there was a box of some sort. He didn't want you to bother with it."

Gillian gulped. She had to think fast. She'd die of embarrassment if the Pierces found out about the cookie box.

"It's in my bag. I'll go get it," she said.

But Mrs. Pierce said, "I'll come with you," and Mary Agatha followed behind her. With two Pierces looking on she fished blindly in the carry-on bag. Her fingers found a little old book she'd bought for Cory, *The Squibob*

61

*Papers.* She handed it shakily to Mrs. Pierce, who held it carefully and turned its pages but looked doubtful.

"I thought Mr. James said—well, I had the idea that it was in a box, and there were—"

"Oh, the box," Gillian said quickly, "it was dirty and I threw it away."

"Well, it's *old*, all right," Mrs. Pierce admitted, "but weren't there some papers?"

"It says 'papers,'" Gillian pointed out demurely, "right in the title." If her father could hear this white lie let him remember that this was a personal emergency.

The important thing was that Mrs. Pierce seemed satisfied. She put the book in a section of her big handbag and closed the zipper. "Let's go, girls," she said confidently and they were on their way.

A single curious incident dimmed the morning. Just as Mrs. Pierce was pulling away from her parking space, Gillian glanced back at the hotel. The maid with the beady eyes and the downy mustache was coming down the service alley.

She was wearing a saggy print dress, not a maid's uniform. And she was swinging her battered purse like a club.

"Fired!" Gillian said out loud, without thinking.

"What?" asked Mary Agatha and her mother in unison.

"Oh, nothing," Gillian said nonchalantly, but she was remembering something. Jojo's house in California had a lot of phones. She would bet anything Jojo had told someone—his secretary or his manager—to phone the Goldcoast East and make the terrible maid go away, even while he was still on the line, with Gillian, pretending everything was cool. It would be just like Jojo to rescue her and say nothing. But what if he hadn't called and she'd answered the door, feeling safe in broad daylight? . . . She glanced back at the maid now stomping purposefully across the street—and shivered.

# 7

She had the window seat. She was feeling as stuffed as the green felt crocodile she kept on her bed at school and equally ready to smile fixedly and foolishly at the world. Chicago and the Goldcoast East were behind her and she wasn't scared about anything. Soon after the FASTEN YOUR SEAT BELT warnings had gone dark, she'd been served a delicious dinner.

Now she took off her shoes and put on the free socks the stewardesses had provided at each seat. Her feet felt okay in the new sneakers, but Jojo ought to get his money's worth whether he knew about it or not. She pushed the button to let the seat back and allowed her head to roll gently against the padding. She wasn't sleepy but she closed her eyes and thought about how great it was to be cruising high above the North Atlantic, with Cory ahead, waiting to meet her in the morning.

The day hadn't been half bad. Mary Agatha had been on her best behavior but just when Gillian had decided to tell her so Mary Ag had said, "I'm certainly glad you were in a good mood today and not all flaky the way you can be."

Could you beat that? But she had hugged Gillian in a truly warm and friendly—very-best-friendly way, and added, "I think you've been super about going so far alone. And you've been just great today."

Well, for Pete's sake, almost anyone acted all right when a mother was in charge, and Mrs. Pierce had been fully in charge of the program. Nicely and politely, as Jojo might say, but with check-reins held firm.

Much of the afternoon the three of them had gone arm in arm, the buddy system as Mrs. Pierce called it.

"We don't want to lose one another while we're browsing and it's an easy thing to do in a crowd this big," she'd said at the art fair.

So no one had gotten lost,. and Mrs. Pierce had kept up the buddy system, which wasn't dumb at all but actually comforting, right up to the moment at O'Hare when Gillian said good-by and promised to write often. She had felt more alone than ever as she walked through the metal detector while a lady searched her carry-on luggage.

She had a little pair of fold-up scissors and a pair of pliers and a short but sturdy screwdriver in her purse. She always carried them, even at school. She had read once about an important New York publisher who had such a bad case of claustrophobia he kept a fire ax in his office washroom. Gillian couldn't very well walk around with a fire ax but she could do the next best thing; and the screwdriver had actually come in handy once when she had to pry herself out of a washroom with a faulty door in the Puerta Vallarta airport.

This evening the airline people, noting these tools, had looked at each other and at her with lifted eyebrows and she had looked stonily at her roommate—out there beyond the glass which separated the public from the passengers. Mary Ag was laughing her head off as usual, but the officials, with straight faces and no remarks, allowed Gillian to board the plane. And no one even questioned her cookie box. She breathed relieved sighs all the way to her seat. If old Mary Ag had known what Gillian was going through she'd have canned her laughter for sure.

So here she was, snug as could be, with only one thing to hamper her comfort. She hadn't followed Jojo's orders about the box. She could still see Mrs. Pierce putting *The Squibob Papers* in her handbag and zipping it carefully into its own compartment.

Jojo had an uncanny way of finding out when you hadn't followed orders, but this time how could it matter? She'd be at Heathrow Airport, London, England, in five or six hours, and Cory would be waiting outside customs. She could go to a ladies' room if she decided to get rid of the box right away. Mrs. Burton's packaging could go into a trash bin and out of her life forever. Even if she hadn't done *exactly* what Jojo said the second time, she was following his original orders—*give the box to Cory and nobody else.*

Having convinced herself she was justified, she felt better, and slid another look at her seatmate.

"My name is Gillian Babcock Saunders," she had said earlier after sitting down.

"Mmmmmm," the girl had said.

"What's your name?"

"Um," the girl said. "Shane McLane."

"I'm from Chicago."

"Yeah." The girl had spoken disinterestedly, as if she and her thoughts were a million miles away. Then she'd added quickly, "Well, I saw you get on. Wasn't that your family waving good-by?"

"Heavens, no. Just friends." But she wasn't displeased that someone thought she had a family to see her off. "I wonder what the movie will be tonight," she'd continued, conversationally.

"Who cares?" Shane McLane had said, closing her eyes.

The girl was about twenty-one, Gillian guessed. She had glossy light brown hair that looked as if she washed it herself, and often, and kept it well brushed, no hair sets, no hair spray. She had gray eyes and thick lashes that might be her own. She had a great complexion too: no freckles, smooth, clear, and lightly tanned like a model's in a cosmetic ad. But, face it, she was a pill not to talk to people.

She hadn't talked to the man across the aisle either. The tanned man who'd been about the last passenger to board the plane. He had the window seat across the aisle, beyond a fat man who was eating or drinking whenever he wasn't dozing. The tanned man had jumped up as soon as the plane was at cruising altitude and asked Shane McLane if she'd like to change places with him.

"Why would I?" she asked indifferently.

"I have the window—you might prefer it."

"To see what?"

"Dawn," he'd said, flashing terribly white teeth. "I hear it's on the schedule." Maybe his grin only looked so white because the rest of him was so brown. *Caps*, Gillian thought, *but not as good as Jojo's.* Jojo was dark too, a whole lot darker than this man—but Jojo's smile was warm and real. I never saw a weasel grin, she thought, but now I know how it might look. Budd was tanned even in winter,

68

but it was a real suntan. *This tan came out of a bottle,* she decided.

Shane McLane must not have liked his smile either.

"Drop dead," she'd told him, and he'd gone back to his seat. Iceberg McLane was asleep now or pretending to be, so Gillian put on her earphones and sampled all the stations. She had a choice of music: country-Western, rock, pop, or classical. Or she could listen to a Spanish lesson. She decided it would be more interesting to finish *Mary Lincoln, One of Ours,* although the author would never be one of her favorites.

It was pretty interesting to be miles above the earth reading about the Widow Lincoln of over a century ago, when air travel was still a pipe dream. Allegedly Mrs. Lincoln, while grieving over her great loss, was dealt an additional burden of outstanding debts, and had sold some of her personal belongings to help clear them. Probably that was when she'd sold the pretty brooch Jojo had bought this summer. Mrs. Lincoln must have parted with many things that were dear to her.

"My word, you're a *real* bookworm," a male voice said. "What's so interesting?"

The tanned man was leaning across Shane McLane, who was awake now but merely staring ahead of her.

"Well, aren't you going to tell me?" he persisted, smiling and smiling. "It must be fascinating—I've been watching you. I wish I had something to keep my mind off where I happen to be right this minute. I'm a terrible coward about planes."

"Oh brother," Shane McLane said, and put on her earphones.

69

The tanned man glanced at her and then gave Gillian a wink.

"It's a book claiming Mary Lincoln was a women's liberator," Gillian said. "It's not very convincing—you can have it." Then realizing how impolite *that* sounded, she added, "I have more books in my bag, if you'd like to see them."

"Would I ever!" he beamed at her. And when she hesitated, remembering Mrs. Burton's cookie box, he said quickly, "I'll be careful. I hate to see anybody mistreat a book."

"I need the other stuff," she said, "but you can have all the books for tonight. I'm going to watch the movie."

"You'll like it. I've seen it. John Wayne, cowboys and rustlers."

The girl beside Gillian stirred impatiently and took off her earphones but held them handy to plug in her ears again. "If you're going to stand there *all* night," she said, "maybe I *had* better switch seats!"

"Oh no!" said the man quickly, clutching Gillian's books to his chest. "I wouldn't disturb you for the world. *Forgive* the intrusion!"

He climbed back over the sleeping fat man. Soon afterward the overhead lights were dimmed, reading lights were flicked on here and there, and a stewardess rolled down the screen.

Economy class had an interesting-sounding French film and you could move back if you wanted to see it, but neither film featured Jojo, even in one of his so-called "cameo" appearances. So Gillian decided to watch the Western. And to heck with Shane McLane.

71

John Wayne finally had it fixed so that all the cattle rustlers and a crooked banker and some other unsavory citizens of Dodge County were either in Boot Hill or in jail, and Gillian drifted into a mixed-up dream in which Mary Lincoln had stolen the Emancipation Proclamation and sold it for a lot of money and then everything was starting to turn out all right because Mrs. Pierce came walking across the dream with a beach bag and said, "Everything seems to be under control. I've got it right here." So they let Mrs. Lincoln go.

And Gillian awoke to find she was clutching her shoulder bag. It was daylight and she was soaring into the rosiest, most splendid dawn she'd ever seen, and this was not a dream. She'd forgot to pull the shade.

Over the loudspeaker the pilot announced rather quietly, probably not to disturb passengers who were still asleep, "We have reached and passed landfall—" and went on to tell those who were awake exactly where they were. But Gillian had to fumble for her handkerchief. She was crying a little. She didn't know why. Maybe, way in the back of her mind, she'd kept on thinking of it as a dangerous ocean. No matter. She had crossed the Atlantic and Mary Kelly's Ireland was somewhere down below and Cory would be just ahead. She dried her tears.

A stewardess whispered, "Good morning," and offered a steaming towel which felt great on Gillian's face. Even Shane McLane opened her eyes and looked grateful for the warm wash-up.

"Hi," Gillian said. "Isn't this a beautiful day?" And leaned back in her seat so Shane could admire the sky. She wanted to talk about a million things and she hoped this

72

girl had decided to be friendly. "Is this your first trip to Europe?" she asked.

"Yeah," said Shane McLane, "and could you draw that shade down? It can't be more than three o'clock in the morning, if that. My watch has stopped."

Gillian drew the shade and hated Shane McLane concentratedly for the next five minutes and kept her own mouth tightly shut. But soon another stewardess handed her a hot breakfast tray, and Gillian, pushing up the shade, said, "I have to see what I'm eating. Sorry."

"Oh, migod!" her seatmate moaned. "At this hour? Wake me when it's over, okay?"

"There's a book or a movie," Gillian said chattily, "called *Wake Me When the War Is Over*. You know it?"

"No," said her seatmate, "but I *love* the idea."

And slept again.

*Or pretended to*, Gillian decided. She also decided to climb over the body and go get cleaned up. She spent a lovely twenty minutes using all the free stuff in the washroom except the shaving equipment. She put an extra toothbrush in her feedbag. Jojo had paid plenty for her ticket. She wouldn't dare give him a toothbrush, though. He'd be sure to figure out where it came from. She could give it to Cory. No pointed questions or accusations from Cory. He had better things on his mind and he trusted her more, at least half the time.

Anyway Cory could have a new toothbrush and the "comfort bag," and maybe someday he'd get his copy of *The Squibob Papers*. Gillian padded down the aisle again to her seat. The tanned man was in Shane McLane's seat and Shane had vanished. "Aren't you the early bird?" he

73

said, showing his dazzling teeth. She sat down and looked out the window.

He had her books in his lap. "I want to thank you for lending me these," he said, patting them gently. "They helped me pass the night. I'm not the world's greatest passenger, you see. Can I put them back in your bag for you?"

"I'll put them back myself," she said.

"It's a most attractive bag," he said, picking it up. "What do you carry in it?" He was smiling broadly but Gillian thought his eyes were cold. Not little black beads, like the maid's, but just as hard.

"Candy bars," she said, belatedly, realizing that she'd been staring at him rudely, "and chewing gum. I should have given you some last night. It's a 'comfort bag' a friend of mine gave me." She took back her purse. "You like comics? I don't. Not often anyway. You want some candy?" She chattered on lightly, packing the books back on top of Mrs. Burton's cookie box.

"No, no thank you," he said hollowly. "Are you traveling by yourself, or with the Ice Princess?"

"By myself," Gillian said and tried to pack ice into her own voice.

"Anybody meeting you?" he asked, and when she failed to answer he added quickly, "It's just that up here I'm a jellyfish but once we're down I can help you with your other bags and find a cab. I feel I owe you something."

"You don't owe me a thing," Gillian said, "and my uncle is meeting me."

Then Shane McLane came back and hesitated beside

74

the seat until the tanned man got up and bowed her into it with a flourish of his hand.

"There's England, I guess," Shane said leaning toward the window. She was looking even prettier than she had last night. And for the first time since she'd come on board she began to chat.

"Your first trip too?" Shane asked.

Gillian nodded, feeling almost unbearably excited, as if she couldn't wait a minute more to land. England! Her heart raced, as patches of land and lakes showed below. Some of the houses still had chimney pots! Just like illustrations in the Mary Poppins books and her long-ago worn-out Mother Goose. Even though you could see superswoosh highways and an airport that seemed to stretch forever, England was still green and tidy!

The plane was down before she could finish tying her shoelaces. The tanned man leaned forward and gave her a Victory signal and called out, "I'll help with your bags, honey!"

Honey! "Yech-h-h!" Gillian said even at this happy moment of arrival.

"Helpful Harry," Shane said. "I meet a lot of them. So will you. Tell you what—let's you and me help each other if there's any helping to be done. And stick close together, okay?"

"Well, sure," Gillian said, surprised by this sudden show of friendliness. "But my uncle's going to be right there— he'll be meeting me—"

"Have you ever *been* to Heathrow?" the girl asked.

"No, but—"

"Neither have I but I've been warned. It's enormous and terribly confusing. If you think it's as easy as walking into O'Hare—like coming home from Mexico—you're wrong. It's a real maze—that's what I hear anyway."

*Like coming home from Mexico* echoed oddly in Gillian's mind, as a stewardess, on the loudspeaker, thanked them for flying this airline and asked them to remain in their seats until the plane had come to a full stop. Gillian had heard it all before—*coming home from Mexico*, in fact. Something shadowy brushed her thoughts but passed by. It *had* to be coincidence. It was nothing at all. But why were two strangers so all-fired anxious to help her walk across an airport and meet Cory? To stick by her? She held fast to her bag, and wondered.

And she was still wondering after she'd stepped off the plane at Heathrow, with Shane McLane and the tanned man following close behind.

# 8

All the while they were going through the business of immigration, passports, and customs declarations and hurrying down to a lower level to watch for their luggage on a big serpentine treadmill, Gillian continued to wonder about Shane McLane. Had Jojo hired her to keep an eye on Gillian as if she were a baby? Shane was pushing the old buddy system all of a sudden. She'd even whispered to Gillian again, "Let's don't get separated. Helpful Harry bugs me."

"What can *I* do?" Gillian had whispered back.

"Isn't your uncle meeting you? Didn't you say that?"

*Not to you*, Gillian thought. But *had* she? She'd told the tanned man, not Shane. At least, she *thought* that was how it had been. She was too excited to keep things straight. She'd be lucky if she could pick out her own bag.

Shane's gray eyes met Gillian's green ones levelly. But it had been Gillian's experience, growing up in boarding schools and camps, that the straightforward look, or approach, was by no means to be trusted at all times.

She wished she could make up her own mind about Shane before Cory met her. Cory never, well, *seldom*, saw anything wrong with people. Not on first acquaintance anyway.

The tanned man was holding Gillian's carry-on case because he had grabbed it in his eagerness to carry it for her. "I wish you girls would tell me what color your bags are. I'll lift them off the runway for you."

"I've only got one," Gillian said. "It's plaid and there are about ten dozen plaid bags going around here. I'll get it when I recognize it."

"Look," he said, his smile as sticky as his words, "we got to be friends last night, right? I owe you a favor—and here we are, three Yanks in a strange country, so let me lend a hand."

"Well, it's only one little old bag," Gillian said.

"For a whole summer in Europe?" he asked sharply.

Who had said a whole summer and whose business was it, she wondered? But there were more important things to think about at the moment. "I sent my trunk straight through," she explained.

His brown eyes studied her. Not warm brown like Jojo's, she thought again, but hard as walnut. Finally he said, "We came straight through, little lady, as straight as the airline flies. So shouldn't we look for your trunk?"

"Of course not, it's on its way to Pisa." It was a good thing Mrs. Pierce had remembered to change its destination to Pisa instead of Paris. In all the excitement Gillian could have forgotten.

"Pisa?" he repeated. "Pisa, Italy?"

"That's what she said," Shane McLane put in testily. And to Gillian, "You just stopping over in London, hon?"

It seemed as if a signal had passed between the girl and the man, but perhaps Gillian was imagining things again. No need to get frightened. Cory was nearby now.

"I'm Karl Dobble," the man said, unexpectedly shoving his hand forward to shake hers. "Karl with a K. We've gotten to be such pals I forget we've never been properly introduced. Let's see, I heard you talking last night, you're Gillian and this is Shane, right?" Pals! Gillian glanced at Shane but the other girl was studying her shoes, her eyelids lowered, her face as still as a mask.

"And now that we're safe on dry land," Dobble continued, "even if it's a foreign land—may I lend a hand with your luggage, little ladies?"

Gillian winced at the "little ladies" stickiness but said, "Here comes mine now. It's got LVs on it. I guess I forgot I didn't bring the plaid one." Papa, forgive the lie.

Dobble promptly plucked her bag from the snaky treadmill as if it were filled with popcorn instead of packed tight with clothes and shoes. He didn't look one tenth as strong as Jojo but he had to be tougher than his slenderness indicated.

"My bag has only *one* set of initials," he pointed out, grinning evilly, or so it seemed to Gillian, guilty with her lie. "But they're my own."

He lifted Shane's blue bag when it arrived and then his own with the gilt-looking K.D. plate on it and carried all three suitcases as if they were empty shopping bags. "Now we'll breeze through customs," he said. "We almost look like a family, don't we?"

For once Gillian took no pleasure in looking like a family. She could hardly wait to get outside, find Cory, and be rid of these two forever. Even in this enormous airport they made her feel as crowded as if they were stepping on her heels. And suddenly she remembered the barber, the waiter,

81

and the maid from the Goldcoast East—all trying to get *at* her it seemed. Maybe it was foolish to think these two strangers were hemming her in, but that was the way she felt. Claustrophobic—almost suffocated! She shook her head and took a deep breath. "I've got to hurry," she said firmly. "My uncle will be waiting."

Almost before she realized it the three of them had breezed through customs, without questions and without any dreaded exposure. She breathed another private sigh of relief. And then from the far edge of a waiting crowd, a familiar voice called, "Nelly Bly! Nelly Bly! Will you pose for pictures?"

Shane said, "Wow! I wonder who the lucky Nelly dame is?" And Gillian said fiercely, "It's me, dummy!"

Later on she could apologize and even explain that Nelly Bly was an old-time girl reporter and world traveler, but right now here was Cory, in golf shirt and slacks looking golden and handsome and carefree.

"You?" Shane gasped. "He looks like Robert Redford—the actor."

"He's my uncle," Gillian said. "He's a sportswriter. I've *got* an uncle who's an actor—" She was chattering, working her way through the crowd, with Shane right at her heels, and Dobble keeping up.

"Well, he's gorgeous," Shane said. "I think I'm beginning to like this—" but cut herself off in mid-sentence.

"Well, good-by now," Gillian hinted, forgetting Dobble still had her luggage.

She flung herself at Cory as if propelled by a slingshot. And then, quickly remembering she was a grown-up, she drew away and said super-casually, "Well, how was the dumb tournament, Cory?"

"It's over," Cory said, grinning. "That's the main thing." He was looking beyond her, smiling, waiting to be introduced to her companions. But Gillian stalled for time. Maybe they'd go away. "Oh my golly!" she said, "I can't believe I'm really in London, England!" and chattered on for a full minute.

"Is one of those Gill's?" Cory finally asked Dobble and introduced himself. "Let me take it."

Gillian had lost control. The three grown-ups were introduced all around and Cory had Gillian's bag in hand and Karl Dobble raised his arm to hail a taxicab.

"Gill and I can take the airline bus into town," Cory protested.

And Gillian said, "Oh, let's! I *love* buses!" An overstatement which caused Cory to give her a long look and all of his attention and thereby lose the argument. Dobble assured them he was on expense account, was taking a taxi anyway, and would enjoy their company if they came along.

Cory relented while Gillian groaned. "That's mighty nice of you." He smiled, depositing Gillian's bags on the sidewalk beside Shane's blue one and Dobble's brown satchel.

"Where are you staying?" Dobble asked Cory.

"The Bartlett. It's small and old-fashioned and I think we'll like it. I left my bag there this morning before I came out."

"Have you been traveling on the Continent?" Dobble was smoother than butter. Smooth as oleo, Gillian thought.

83

Cory said he'd been in Muirfield, Scotland, covering the British Open, which led into a discussion of golf. And Gillian, hating Cory's friendliness with creepy smoothy Dobble, interrupted them, "Did any of you know that Mary Lincoln had eighty-four pairs of glasses?"

"And sixty crates of household goods when she left the White House," Cory said promptly.

"Oh golly, that reminds me—" but Gillian bit her lip and said no more. Dobble took a sudden interest in her words. "Yes, Gillian? Something reminds you—"

"How did we get from the tenth tee to the Lincolns?" Cory asked innocently. "At any rate, in the sandtrap—"

"Never mind," Dobble cut him off, looking strangely red under the tan. "What were you saying, Gillian?"

But Shane spoke up now. "Gillian could I talk to you alone for just half a second?" And led her almost forcefully away from the two men.

Out of earshot Shane still spoke in a whisper, "I don't want that Dobble to know where I'll be, Gillian. Listen, is it all right if I tell him I'm staying at your hotel and wait there until he's gone? Please, can I? I don't know a soul in this whole country except you."

"Except me?" Gillian gasped. "Then why are you here?" she wanted to ask. Shane didn't look like a carefree traveler on a vacation; she had only one little lightweight bag. She certainly wasn't an international hitchhiker, and she didn't talk like a college girl who might be coming to school here.

"I'll explain later," Shane promised, "but I would appreciate it if I could stay with you until he's gone."

84

"Oh, okay," Gillian said. "No big deal."

"I'll make it up to you later," Shane promised.

Don't, thought Gillian.

Cory and Dobble were comparing golf handicaps and didn't seem to notice that the ladies had rejoined them until Gillian announced, "Hey, guess what? Miss McLane is at the Bartlett, too." She winked at Cory and tried to convey a covert message to him, but he only grinned and winked back, oblivious.

Cory was really stubborn that way. When you were telling him something gossipy he'd usually say, "Speak up, I can't hear you." He claimed that his eardrum had been damaged by a mine explosion during the war, and his hearing wasn't up to par any more. But he could hear just fine when you didn't want him to.

Gillian gave up in despair, and in another moment Dobble announced, "Here comes a cab now, folks."

The taxicab, jet black and gleaming, pulled up to the curb and idled as passengers and baggage were deposited inside. Gillian couldn't have been more excited about a presidential limousine. It was so big inside you could just about walk into it standing up. "I love it, I love it!" she said to Cory. "It's so *English!* Raffles, or Basil Rathbone, Sherlock Holmes and Dr. Watson rode in these. I've seen'm a million times!"

Dobble, ignoring her excitement, said, "To the Bartlett, please," and the driver answered, "Yes, indeed, mate." And they were off to Londontown, to the real thing, at last!

Gillian stared in disbelief as they passed an automobile. "Oh my golly, look at that!" she squeaked, pointing. "The driver's asleep!" Cory smiled at her. "The driver is on the other side, Gill. His passenger is asleep. You'll get used to it."

"I can't wait to see everything!" she announced.

"What you'll see first is the sack," Cory said. "For at least three hours, then we'll take a look around."

"I can recommend the Connaught for dinner," Dobble volunteered. "It's very near your hotel, but you'll need to make reservations."

"We like to mess around and find things for ourselves," Gillian said, and then blushed because Cory was giving her a look that warned, "Knock it off." She lapsed into silence, but her spirits weren't dampened. Not in the least. It was all so new and exciting. The double-decker buses, the policemen on horseback; the fountains and the stores and the steep-gabled row-houses dazzled her. "Where are we now?" she wanted to know.

"That's Hyde Park," Cory said, sharing her excitement. "We're coming into Mayfair."

Dobble, seated on one of the jump seats, had begun to drum impatiently on his knee. He said, "I'll be keeping the cab, and of course I insist on paying. Here's Berkeley Square. We're almost there now."

Gillian sensed that suddenly Dobble couldn't wait to be *rid* of his announced buddies. As soon as the cab came to a full stop by a cozy-looking hotel on Curzon Street, Dobble scrambled out to shake hands all around. Then he quickly slid back in the cab and called, "See you around!"

"Not if we see you first," Shane muttered, and for once Gillian agreed wholeheartedly.

But just the same she watched the car go, finding it

curious that Dobble had dumped them so fast. And now he had leaned forward to talk at length to the driver. Where he had to go, Gillian surmised, must be far off the beaten track. She frowned in thought, but was interrupted by Cory. "Hey, Gill," he said, "the idea is to doze off in your room, not here in the middle of the street." But Gillian wasn't dozing. And wouldn't doze, she decided, until Shane McLane was gone.

# 9

Cory's room was ready but Gillian's was not. Shane said quickly that she was perishing for a cup of tea and asked them to join her in the hotel parlor.

"I'll have tea," Cory said, "but maybe Gillian had better go ahead and sack out in my room."

"No way," Gillian said. "I didn't come millions of miles just to sleep."

To make sure of it, she ran ahead of them to the hotel lounge and found a comfortable sofa with space enough for three. Surely this room was in every British film she'd ever seen. She recognized and loved every inch of it: the warm wood walls, golden brown chairs of real leather, and lamps of solid brass, and the carpet was the deepest red she'd ever seen. "Where's the bar or the tea table?" she whispered to Cory.

He smiled. "The British are very proper people," he said. "A waiter will come to take our order."

"I love it, love it, love it," she said blissfully.

She wanted to reach out and hug the lady with her hat on and writing a letter at a big oak desk, the whiskered man in a woolly sweater who was reading his morning newspaper and drinking his tea without looking at the cup, or even the saucer when he put it down again. They were so *proper*. So—so British!

"I'll have tea," she said quickly before Cory could order milk. "And maybe Shane would like some booze—I mean a cocktail. That is, another cocktail." As Shane's mouth opened in astonishment, Gillian added kindly, "You only had one, as I remember."

Shane's mouth hung open but she said nothing.

"Cory doesn't drink," Gillian explained. "And he rarely remembers to order a cocktail for someone else."

"Rarely," Cory agreed, "at five or six o'clock in the morning. I've lost count of the time change—"

"I haven't," Shane said at last, "and I had my drink only ten hours ago. So I'll have tea, with cream and sugar," she said, smiling pointedly at Gillian.

"Well, old Dobble is gone," Gillian said, "and he must be staying a long way off. It took him a whole block to tell the driver where to go."

Shane gave her a pleading look. "I hope you won't mind if I wait for the cup of tea—I'm more tired than I thought, but I don't want to be a pest—" Before they could say stay or go, she had jumped up and announced, "I'll phone my hotel to see if my room is ready. Back in a jiff!"

"Jiff!" echoed Gillian. "Can you imagine anyone saying 'Back in a jiff' in London, England?"

But Cory looked grave. "Gill, how did you manage to grow into such a smart alec in only thirteen years? What's gotten into you? You'd think this Shane girl had just swiped your allowance. And I thought you said she was staying here—"

"She just said that to keep away from Karl Dobble."

"I can buy that," Cory said.

"Tell me about Budd's house," Gillian said. "I can't wait to see it."

Cory was still relating what he knew about the house in Tuscany when Shane returned, looking disturbed. "There's been an awful mix-up." she said. "The hotel has never heard of me, and the clerk doesn't know of an empty room in London."

"We'll ask this clerk," Cory said.

"I did. Nothing! Not even a broom closet—I don't know what to do!"

"Go to the American Embassy," Gillian said. "It's what everybody does in books." And when Cory gave her a look, she snapped, "You're *supposed* to, I bet!" Cory ignored her and asked McLane if she had any friends in London.

"Only Gillian," Shane said.

Gillian gritted her teeth and slurped the last of her lukewarm tea.

"I know it's very unusual," Shane was looking down in synthetic shame, but Cory was listening sympathetically. Since *he* didn't go around making up stories he never suspected anyone else. Not anyone over thirteen, anyway.

"I didn't want to talk about it, but the truth is—my mother died. She was sick for a long, long time, and I promised her I would go somewhere—just pack and go, take all the vacations I missed when—when I had to be with her. She was so brave." Here a tear escaped and rolled slowly down a pale cheek. Could it have been real? wondered Gillian. "I didn't want to spoil *your* holiday talking about sad things. I'm sorry and I won't stay any longer. The desk clerk asked me to tell you your room is ready."

Gillian frowned, suddenly uncertain. *Nobody* would lie about her mother! Anything else maybe but not about a mother dying. She mumbled, "I'm sorry. My mother died, too, a long time ago." And looked at the fingernails she was trying not to bite these days and wondered if she should offer Shane half her room.

She was still considering the possibility when Cory said, "Your room will surely have two beds in it, *acushla*. We'll check to be sure. You don't mind having company until we can find something for Shane, do you?" It was more of an order than a request.

Gillian sighed and covered her dismay with a yawn. "I guess not," she managed finally.

As they headed for the elevators, she made a stab at regaining control of the situation. Let it be known that she was the willing hostess here, not someone backed into a corner. "I'm sure you're welcome to stay all afternoon," she told Shane. "Hey, Cory, what was the new name you called me—*acushla?* They all call me names," she boasted.

"It's Irish," Cory said. "It means 'pulse of the heart'— puts me one up on Budd, doesn't it? He won't know that one."

"I wouldn't bet on it," Gillian said.

"Neither would I." Cory grinned. "It'll be good to see old *padrone* Greenburg, won't it? The Italian householder —How do you say 'What time is breakfast?' in Italian?"

"*Quién sabe?*" said Gillian, and giggled because every- thing was *simpático* again.

The room was old, as expected, and spacious and pleas- ant. Even the bathroom was vast, with high ceilings and windows and a giant tub on claw-foot legs that was much older than the shower it now supported. The fixtures were genuine old-fashioned porcelain, and even the floor tiles were real, not linoleum.

Gillian thought it would be nice to soak in that gunboat of a tub, but decided to wait until Shane McLane was on her way.

"How darling!" Shane was saying to Cory as she gazed about the bedroom. "Even the windows have petticoats. And it's so *big*. At least I won't be crowding Gillian." You bet your boots you won't, Gillian thought.

But when the two girls were left alone Gillian began to doubt her fears and regret her attitude. She was probably all wrong about Shane; maybe the girl really *had* lost her mother and was just trying to "forget."

"You can use the bath first," Gillian offered.

But Shane said she'd just slip off her shoes and her jacket and lie down on whichever bed Gillian didn't want—for a few minutes only and then she'd be on her way.

"I'll probably be gone when you wake up, so let me thank you again. And I hope you have a great summer."

"You, too," Gillian said. "And I'm sorry about your mother. I really am."

Shane looked momentarily stunned. Maybe Gillian shouldn't have mentioned her loss; she hoped Shane wouldn't start crying. "I can't wait to see everything," she said quickly. "Cory ought to know I'm not an old lady. I don't have to go to bed in the middle of the morning!"

"I think your uncle will be disappointed if you don't try, Gillian. Why don't you sit in a hot tub for a while and get into your pajamas. I'll order some hot chocolate. It'll do us both good."

"Okay, I'll sit in the tub," Gillian said. Pajamas in the morning, yuck! But she had to change her clothes anyway for tonight and maybe Shane was right for once. Cory wouldn't budge out of this hotel for sure unless he thought she'd slept so she might as well give it a try.

She unlocked her suitcase and got her pajamas and took them into the bathroom along with her handbag.

The bath had been a good idea. When she had rubbed herself down with the biggest towel and gotten into her pajamas and gone back to the bedroom, the hot chocolate was on the night table.

"You'd better drink it fast," Shane advised. "I'm afraid it's getting cold. I've already had mine."

Gillian tasted it. It was warm and rich and chocolaty, and she drank it all.

Shane had put a traveling alarm clock—set for an hour from now—on the night table. She was lying on the bed closest to the window with her suit jacket and her shoes off. "I won't use the alarm if you think it might wake you," she offered. "I'm just going to rest anyway."

"*Nothing* wakes me," Gillian said. "I slept through a burglary in our apartment and once a house burned down right next to the camp I was in and I was the only one that didn't see it."

She flopped down on the vacant bed. She had suddenly begun to feel very drowsy. She fought it, but her eyelids drooped heavily and refused to stay open. "Sleepy," she breathed. "Mm," answered Shane.

"Town Bug bought 'is housin c'called Cammyoor . . ."

In the haze of a dream Shane McLane arose from the bed and floated across the room to where the suitcases lay,

95

striking Gillian's repeatedly till it gaped open and Gillian's clothes rose and danced in mid-air. Gillian struggled to speak; to leap from the bed and retrieve her crazed belongings, but her tongue was leaden; her body not her own.

# 10

The transatlantic phone call took considerable time, but that was to be expected. And Dobble had plenty of time. He smiled. Not dazzlingly this time, but craftily. A sinister smile that suited a sinister plan. For Dobble was a fake. A trumped-up nice guy who not twenty-four hours ago was the scheming Kurt Durkin. He leaned lazily against the phone booth and inspected his fingernails. If Shane McLane had followed his instructions young Miss Saunders would be sleeping like the dead. Cory Moore was safely shackled where he'd be of no help to anyone, and when Durkin had his hands on the box he would decide what next to do with the gullible Mr. Moore. By then it would be a doped sports-writer's babbling testimony against that of a clear-thinking scholar. Who would believe Moore's delusions of kidnaping? The only witnesses would favor Durkin. For Durkin was a very persuasive man.

So far everything had gone as planned. McLane had been convincing in her role—which was more than one might expect from a third-rate T.V. actress. She'd handled the Saunders girl perfectly. With friendliness, yet reserve. And she would take the luggage apart, if necessary, before the brat ever woke up.

It was a quarter of an hour before Mattson was on the

line from Chicago. He was convinced, he said, that the box was not in America but in England.

"That girl has it tucked away somewhere and it's your job to find it, Durk."

"What makes you so certain?" Durkin barked. "What about that Pierce woman? How carefully did you investigate her?"

"Pete followed the Pierces on the bus to the parking lot. Frisked them both and found nothing. All the woman had on her was an old humor book—a dog—printed about mid-1860s. Old, but worthless. Planted, most likely, to fool us."

"What about a false cover?"

"Pete checked it out. No go."

"What about their car?"

"What about it? The boys went over it with everything but a divining rod. Don't fret about this end, Durkin—start worrying about yours!"

"Just how soon can we expect the Pierce woman to squawk to James?"

"In the first place she's got nothing to squawk *about*. Pete's no amateur. He lifted their wallets and *left* the book and picked up three extra wallets on that busload including the driver's. They won't connect the action with the Saunders kid. Not a chance."

Mattson sighed a costly ten seconds before continuing, "In the second place, James has gone on location somewhere in Mexico that can only be reached by mule pack or helicopter. *He* won't be a problem till you get back. Then, boy, *you'd* better be prepared—"

"I haven't laid a finger on the girl!" Durkin warned. "You remember that!"

"Oh, *I'll* remember. *You* better hope *she* remembers."

Durkin changed the subject. "There's the outside chance, of course, that she shipped the box to Pisa."

"What do you mean, Pisa? Italy?" Mattson's voice was shrill. "My idiot brother-in-law said she was supposed to give it directly to her Uncle Cory. In London!"

Durkin took a deep breath and explained the change in travel plans as best he could. Mattson was not convinced.

"You might have inspected that luggage yourself, you know. What's holding you back, Kurt? Do you realize what's at *stake* here?"

"I'm reasonably certain it's not in her luggage, T.D., I think she's wearing it." Kurt Durkin was holding his temper by a slender thread.

"Wearing it!" Mattson sneered. "I have a sneaking suspicion you never even tried to search those bags. Don't think you're not in this as deep as the rest of us."

Then Durkin exploded, "Listen, you ignoramus! You know as well as I do why I hired that crummy actress to do the prying for me. If I so much as touch that girl I'll get the book thrown at me for child molesting. You stupid fool! You know and every cop in Chicago knows that's what got me sent up before!"

Mattson's voice sounded placating at the other end of the line. "Okay, Durk, okay." He went on. "Saunders carries a purse, doesn't she?"

"Yes, indeed, a thing she slings over her shoulder and never takes off. Not even a dumb kid would keep any-

99

thing valuable in an open feedbag. It doesn't even fasten shut."

"Did McLane have a chance to go through it?" Mattson persisted.

"No, but she saw the contents. She was right on Saunders' tail at O'Hare, watching as *they* searched. Are you ready for this? She's got a pair of pliers and a screwdriver; a hairbrush, Kleenex. No lipstick, no cosmetics of any kind. And all she's got in the satchel are books and sweets: cookies, candy, chewing gum, comics! It must be hidden in her underwear. It's the only place left. McLane will find it."

"You call me the minute that happens, Durk."

"Yes, indeed," said Durkin, a slow smile spreading across his face. "It won't be long now. The kid's got no way out."

"Okay," Mattson said. "And maybe *you* better think about heading for cover when this is over. Doc Sawyers is out to find who hired three guys to toss him around and bruise his ribs that day at the airport. Somebody says he's got the whole Bears backfield helping him look."

"With the money this deal will bring, I can buy my own football team, or an army, if I need it," Durkin bristled. "And maybe you'd better take a month in the country if your nerves are going bad!" Then he hung up.

# 11

She was on a roller coaster going down. Then it was a Ferris wheel letting off passengers, start, stop, bump, and all the seats rocking wildly. "Get off, get off!" the operator was saying, but she was at the top of the wheel and it was a long way to the ground. "Get up, get up" the voice begged her. "*Wake up*, Gillian, *please!*"

*Wake* up! That was it. She opened her eyes, afraid to see how far away the ground might be.

She was in bed—in her pajamas—in a strange room. A room with ruffled curtains and chintz draperies and somebody was shaking her violently. "Gillian, please, look at me!" Somebody seemed to be swearing softly and sobbing at the same time. "Gillian, sit up!"

The room reeled as Gillian sat up too fast. "Oh my golly!" She held her throbbing head. "What's the matter with me?" She saw that Shane's face was tear-streaked. "And what's the matter with *you?*"

"Never mind," Shane said, looking a little less scared. "Will you get dressed and make it snappy?"

Gillian gazed fuzzily toward the windows. It was still daylight. "Must've dozed off," she mumbled. Her throat was parched and her ears were ringing. She shook her head to clear it but the pounding got worse. "I'd better tell Cory I'm awake." She groped for the phone, but Shane said, "It's no use. He's gone."

Gillian's thoughts seemed as blurred as her vision. Maybe this was the jet lag everyone talked about. "Um. Gone. So where do we meet him?"

"He's *gone*, Gillian. He's not in London—do you understand? Now get dressed and hurry, will you, please?" Shane was firm but obviously impatient.

Gillian took the phone in both hands and dialed with trembling fingers. "Please ring Mr. Corydon Moore's room," she asked the operator.

"Mr. Moore has checked out," the operator said promptly.

"He couldn't have!" Gillian cried. "I'm here!" But the operator asked her to hold the line for a moment. A crisp male voice told her that Mr. Moore's friend had checked out for him yesterday. No message had been left. The voice assured her courteously that her charges had been paid but the room must be made available by one o'clock.

She hung up slowly and stared fixedly at Shane. "He said yesterday! But that's crazy!"

Shane avoided her eyes.

"We got here almost twenty-four hours ago," she said. "And you've had a nice long rest. So get moving. We're going to Italy and find your Uncle Budd. Heathrow is a good hour's drive from here so try to hurry, will you?"

*Where's Cory?* Gillian screamed, but only in her still-aching head. She drew her knees up to her chest and held herself jackknifed as if the bed might slip away like a raft caught in a whirlpool. As if she might spring apart like a broken watch. Four years ago there'd been a terrible morning when she woke to find tear-streaked faces and no one wanting to look at her or tell her the truth.

She put her forehead against her knees and pressed the hurt in. Then she faced Shane again and said, "Whatever's happened—you'd better tell me."

Shane kept on looking at the ceiling. "Cory had to go back to Scotland. One of the golfers got caught cheating on a scorecard and Cory had to go cover the scandal. He asked me to take you to Budd. I've got your ticket and money for expenses so we can take a cab to the airport if you'll just get a move on."

"Well, all right!" Gillian yelled, letting out her breath with a great whoop of relief. "Why didn't you say so in the first place!" If Cory was okay, she could stand almost anything. Even having drippy old Shane McLane around all the way to Italy.

Gillian could dress with the speed of a fireman if she felt the need to. She raced into her clean underwear, new jeans, a shrink top, and her sneakers. Within minutes she was ready to leave but she told Shane, "I'd really like to call Jojo and let him know our plans are changed—"

"No!" Shane said sharply.

Gillian said, "I'd call collect—he'd pay for it, if *that's* what's worrying you."

*Something* was worrying Shane McLane, it was obvious from her scowl. She was deep into her own thoughts the same as she'd been on the plane from Chicago, but the problem wasn't money.

"I don't care who pays—we simply haven't got time! We've *got* to get out of London. I mean—" her gray eyes focused on Gillian for a minute. "I thought you were anxious to see your Uncle Budd!"

"Well, I do want to see Budd," Gillian said, as soon as they were in the taxicab, "but he's not my real uncle. They're all my guardians." Free to abandon you at any time and—it was now evident—anywhere.

"Are you all right?" Shane asked. "You still look glassy-eyed."

"I'm Alice through the looking glass," Gillian decided. It was an Alice kind of day—a world where things floated. . . . "But if there's no meaning in it," said the King, "that saves a world of trouble as then we needn't look for any." She pondered the words of Lewis Carroll. Okay then, she wouldn't look for trouble. But she wished she could have squared herself with Jojo, apologize for not following his orders. And not giving the box to Cory, either! She'd forgotten all about it and now she'd have to take it to Pisa. But maybe Budd would take charge of it then. No big worry.

"Good-by, Piccadilly," she said, as the cab turned a corner in Berkeley Square. "I'll bet we're the only visitors to London, England, that never even saw it. Farewell, Berkeley Square! Aren't there supposed to be nightingales singing around here?"

Shane said, "Just cool it, please. Next you'll be bawling."

Just look who's talking about bawling, thought Gillian, remembering Shane's tears. Was Shane crying about her mother this morning? Or was something else bothering her?

"How long does this trip to Pisa take?"

"I don't really know—we're not going there directly."

Shane answered evasively and Gillian cast a sharp glance at her.

"*I* am going to Pisa," said Gillian, "and nowhere else." Was Shane up to something? Gillian didn't want to believe it. This morning Shane had seemed a whole lot friendlier than yesterday. But she also looked just a little furtive and worried about something and very, very uncertain.

"We're going by way of Milan," Shane said, "that's because your uncle—your guardian—planned to show you the museums. That's the way your ticket reads and mine has to match if I'm your escort, right? And I promised him I'd deliver you to Budd Greenburg." Sensible enough, Gillian thought, but she couldn't help feeling there was something more that Shane was holding back.

"Well, cheer up," she advised. "You'll love Budd. All the girls do. Everywhere. Chicago, Mexico, Europe . . ."

"Oh, knock it off," Shane said impatiently. "We'll probably be able to rent a car in Pisa and then we can look for this Camaiore and ask somebody how to find the house. There can't be too many lovers named Budd Greenburg in a town nobody ever heard of."

"Just wait till you meet him, you'll change your tune!"

She lapsed into brooding silence.

As they waited in the airport section for departing continental passengers, Shane explained that there were no seat reservations on this flight, no first or second class. "So we'll have to listen and run for it." She meant listen and try to decipher the announcements coming steadily and confusingly over a blaring and altogether unclear loudspeaker.

"I can't understand anything they're saying," Gillian confessed.

"Just concentrate on the flight number," said Shane, "and getting on that plane."

It would have been simple except that a horde of Japanese tourists suddenly arrived, chattering and bustling excitedly at the gates. They were pretty much the same size, no taller than Gillian and just as thin, with the exception of one plump lady and two robust elderly gentlemen. Gillian watched them with envy. "They're having *fun*," she said. "They all look so happy."

"And well dressed," Shane added. "They must be on a tour. Let's hope to heaven they're not on *our* plane."

The loudspeaker crackled information and Shane yelled, "That's it—here we go!"

Shane grabbed for Gillian's hand, but a smiling Japanese girl slipped between them. She was followed by three more.

"You're offside!" Gillian yelled, which was something Jojo sometimes hollered when watching a football game on T.V. Jojo would have enjoyed a scrimmage like this and nobody would have got ahead of him. Shane, somewhere behind her, was calling, "Get two seats!" as Gillian rushed forward.

The Japanese filled most of the plane and Gillian hurrying down the aisle bumped into a tall pale man who was wearing wrap-around sunglasses, so dark you could only see your own reflection in them. He quickly stepped aside and merely nodded at her hasty, "Excuse me!"

The last two seats in the plane were the only ones left. It would be a bumpy ride back here but she didn't care. She was on her way to Italy and Budd and that was all that mattered.

Shane flung herself into the seat beside Gillian. "Boy, oh boy, am I ever out of shape! As soon as I get through with this job—trip—I'm going to start jogging again."

"What job?" Gillian asked.

Shane looked away quickly and sighed. "Look, can't we just can the conversation for a while? I'm winded."

Okay, Gillian thought. She wouldn't talk. But nobody could keep her from thinking, and her thoughts all led to one conclusion. Shane was up to something. And Gillian Babcock Saunders would keep her eyes open. The anxious way Shane looked meant it couldn't be anything good.

After O'Hare and Heathrow the Milan airport seemed small, but the terminal was just as busy. Gillian had to go to the ladies' room and Shane was left to watch for both their bags.

"Don't worry," Shane told her. "Just hurry up and be back to help carry the stuff through customs."

Gillian hurried, taking her carry-on bag with her. It now held three cookie boxes, two real, one not. On the flight from London each passenger had been given a sample box of Italian cookies and Shane had promptly said, "I notice you collect freebies; add this. I don't like sweets."

"I don't like cookies either!" Gillian had snapped and then felt her face burn. "I mean for breakfast!"

She'd left her comfort bag of candy bars and gum at the Bartlett in lieu of a tip, because her cellophane sack of British money was missing. She didn't remember taking it out of her purse but anything could happen on this weird journey. It wasn't worth worrying about so long as Cory had given Shane funds to cover everything. She could tell Jojo about it later and maybe he'd take it out of her allowance.

Washing her hands in the ladies' room she took mental inventory. She had cookies and her Mary Lincoln books and Cory's box plus her papers, traveler's checks, hardware, and brushes. Everything was under control but her dumb tongue, saying she didn't like cookies. Shane hadn't seemed to notice, though.

She jogged across the lower level of the terminal toward the stairs. You couldn't find your best friend in this colorful, noisy, shoving crowd, she thought, and then her heart bumped. Someone familiar stood at the foot of the stairs!

But she was mistaken. For a split second she'd thought the man was Karl Dobble. But it was only the tall pale man she'd bumped against in the plane. Even so she ducked behind two college boys with knapsacks on their backs. She didn't want to face anyone who even looked like Dobble.

About half the airport crowd seemed to be speaking English but Gillian could pick out snatches of Italian, French, Spanish, and German. Budd would have been proud.

Shane was waiting beside their bags, impatient to go through customs. Gillian stopped before meeting her to give a box of cookies to a little girl. The girl looked down bashfully but her mother smiled and thanked her. *"De nada,"* said Gillian a bit uncertainly. *"Di nulla, prego—"*

A crowd of people surged toward the gates for the plane to Pisa. Gillian and Shane moved along as best they could, bumping their bags against their legs; obviously they hadn't got the knack of international shoving. They were learning, though.

They had just about caught up with the man in the black shades. He was towering over the crowd. "Does that tall guy remind you of Dobble?" Gillian whispered to Shane. And Shane suddenly looked even paler than the stranger.

"I think I'm going to be sick," she moaned, holding her stomach. And Gillian believed her. She looked awful.

"If we hurry and board the plane you can use an airsick bag," Gillian offered, but Shane had already headed for the terminal's nearest rest room.

# 12

Shane was in the rest room for some time, and emerged apologizing. "I'm sorry," she said, "about everything."

"It's all right. We can always catch another plane. You going to have a baby or something?"

Shane stared, then threw back her head and laughed heartily for the first time in their forty-odd hour acquaintance. "You really are the darnedest kid!" she said. "Let's find out where we can hire some wheels."

She led the way upstairs to a rent-a-car desk.

"If Durkin's here it's because he's following us," Shane said. "I think I should tell you that."

"Durkin who?" Gillian demanded. "You mean the guy in the dark glasses? You know him?"

"Durkin is his real name," Shane said tiredly. "Durkin is Dobble. And obviously he's quit using that suntan makeup."

Gillian nodded glumly, realizing she wasn't really surprised.

"Is he your boy friend?" she asked uneasily. "Is that why you're running away from him?" But Shane had said *following us!* Let it be a mistake! Let it be Shane old Durkin-Dobble was chasing! And let Gillian Babcock Saunders get to Budd. This was Budd's country—and she could find him. Even if she had to walk, or swim, or hitch a ride.

"Listen," Shane said, "let's get ourselves a car and then we'll talk, okay?"

"Have I got a choice?" Gillian asked nasty-sweet. But she tagged after Shane. The rent-a-car man was young and helpful, and more than willing to show Shane how to use the levers and buttons on the hired Fiat. He warned her that all Italia was a traffic hazard in midsummer. Bumper to bumper in the cities and no speed limits in open country except where posted.

"Wouldn't it have been faster to wait for the next plane?" Gillian asked.

"No, and anyhow we don't want to go anywhere near Pisa, if Durkin's there. Camaiore is *this* side of Pisa—look at the map. Durkin will be waiting at the airport. He'll probably try to get at your trunk. Lord knows he can wheel and deal but it's a foreign country and that ought to slow him down. Now where in blazes is the ignition? What does the manual say?"

Gillian held the Fiat manual open to a double-page spread of the dashboard and equipment. "*Pedale del gas? L'accensione?*"

The young man, who had been leaning on the hood drawing an accessory map to lead them out of the city, came back in time to hear her. He said she had a fine accent, and would they, please, observe the road signs he had sketched to lead them onto the Aurelian Way—Via Aurelia, from Roman times, he added.

"It's a highway and it goes south, right?" Shane asked.

"*Si, signorina!*"

"Roman times," Shane muttered. "If the traffic is all he

says, Ben Hur could have beat us to Camaiore—at least the horses knew the way."

"*Signorina,* you know the necessary road signs?"

"No," Shane groaned. "I hear they'll soon be universal, but not soon enough."

"They look easy—most of them," Gillian pointed out. "Here's a telephone—and the one with a wrench and pump is a gas station."

The young man said there were places to stop for gas or food on the autostrada. "You have no problems, *signorina.*"

"I'll bet," said Shane.

Gillian said, "You've been very kind. Thanks. *Gràzie molto!*"

"*Non c'e di che!* Bye, bye."

Shane smiled. "You're a real linguist, aren't you?"

"Hardly," Gillian admitted. "I only know a few words."

"Let's hope they're the right ones," Shane said and gritted her teeth. She was trying to maneuver the Fiat through a snarl of little cars, Vespas, bicycles, a mule-drawn cart, and pedestrians darting into every open space.

"I suppose you're sure Dobble—Durkin—is looking for us—both of us—" Gillian began, but Shane, hugging the wheel, said, "Just save the small talk till I get the hang of this rat race."

"What does he want?" Gillian persisted. "What do *you* want?"

Shane started and the car swerved onto the shoulder. She eased it back while Gillian waited.

"You're in it, too, whatever it is," Gillian said. "So what are you up to?"

Shane said something under her breath and kept her eyes on the road. Again Gillian had to curb her impatience, but nothing could stop her from thinking out loud. "I guess everything started to get flaky way back at the Goldcoast East," she announced. "Even before Jojo left—that creepy old barber was a snoop. And there was a waiter that acted weird, and a maid that looked like a battleship." She sent a sidelong glance at Shane. "Did you ever meet any of those people?"

Shane's face reddened. "I was supposed to keep an eye on you. That's all—just about all I've done! I don't even want your stupid box!"

Gillian sat up sharply. "Cory's box! I knew it!" Then she corrected herself. "I just about knew it anyway!"

"It belongs to Durkin," Shane said. "Durkin and his partner Mattson. I don't know what's in it or why they want it so badly, and I couldn't care less. All I want to do now is deposit you at Budd Greenburg's house and split. Durkin is a screwy guy—I think he's crazy—and he might do *anything* to get what he wants!"

She pointed suddenly at a road sign. "Quick, Gill! What does that mean? *Pass* or *Don't pass?*"

They were zinging around what might be called a hairpin curve, but a hairpin that had got caught in a mixer.

"I can't find it," Gillian said, scanning the map and the symbols, "but it must mean *pass*, everybody's going around us! No, wait—it means *Intersection with Side Road* or else it's *Closed Except to Motorcycles—*"

"Oh, shut up," Shane said, "and keep that seat belt tight. What I wish is I'd never told that rent-a-car man where we wanted to go! I should have said Rome or

114

Venice—anywhere but Camaiore. Durkin will phone the place as soon as he discovers we aren't on the next plane. And you can bet your boots he'll get the make and even the license number of this car. How could I be so dumb!"

"Speaking of dumb," Gillian said, "how did you get mixed up with such a creep in the first place?"

Shane's cheeks still burned with embarrassment.

"I'm an actress," she said, "and I've been out of work a long time. I was afraid if something didn't come up soon I'd have to go home." Home, she added, was Bethany, Missouri, a great place for horses and cows but nowhere for a television actress. "So when Dobble—Durkin—offered me a free trip to Europe and a fat commission just to find his box, well, how could I turn him down?"

"Well, you should have known it was a shady deal," Gillian said. "You would've had to *steal* from me. And somebody could have been hurt."

"Of course I know it was wrong *now*. But Durkin did give orders not to harm you. That's why you haven't been grabbed and searched right down to your belly button. He's got a real thing about it. He doesn't want to get too close to you."

Gillian didn't want to think about Dobble—or Durkin—tan or pale—getting anywhere near her ever again, but she said stubbornly, "It's Jojo's box—he paid for it. And it'll be Cory's as soon as I can give it to him."

Shane sighed wearily. "Durkin has a partner named Mattson. They own a store called the Roudy Goudy and your Jojo must have picked up this box by mistake when he was buying something else. There's something very valuable in it and Durkin intends to get it back, believe me!"

"Jojo bought it at an antique store—he goes there all the time. The owner is a very old man and he's honest! Jojo told me so. You ought to be ashamed of yourself believing liars and working for people who steal things! Hey—" she added softly, "does your mother still live in Bethany, Missouri?"

Shane said, "Sure, why?" Then recalling her lie about *that*, she blushed again. "I'm sorry, I truly am."

The Fiat rounded a curve and the road peeled away around them.

After a mile or so of silence, Gillian asked, "Is Durkin really crazy?"

"I don't know. He gets a strange look in his eye sometimes. He warned me to take it very, very easy with you. And when he fired that hulk of a maid he nearly choked her. I think he's afraid of his own violence."

"Has she got a mustache?" Gillian shrieked.

"Maybe. I only saw her once. It was the same day Durkin hired me—she came into the bookstore and tried to tell him she couldn't get anything out of you."

Gillian shivered. She had been right to be scared, after all!

"You tied a can to her tail, anyway, Gill. She got the ax."

"Jojo is very smart about doors and extra locks and just about everything," Gillian said soberly. "And I wish he was here this minute."

The two girls were cruising through some of the greatest countryside Gillian had ever seen. She wished she could enjoy it. "How did you meet Durkin in the first place?"

she asked, trying to get everything straight. "He wouldn't hire just any actress, would he?"

"Mattson is my roommate's uncle. She's got a tiny brain but a big heart. She was just trying to help me out. She didn't know any more than I did that it was anything dishonest." Shane steered over onto the shoulder as three Italian sports cars ripped past.

"Why did he wear that dumb suntan stuff?" Gillian asked. "It didn't even look real."

"If you ask me it was to hide prison pallor," Shane answered. "I'm not sure but I'd bet anything he's been in jail or worse. I guess now he just doesn't care how he looks—all he wants is that box!"

"Well, what makes everybody think *I've* got it!" Gillian snapped. "You must have looked through everything while I was asleep."

Shane said meekly. "I did go through your things. I searched your handbag and your luggage two or three times. But I couldn't find a trace of it."

"Because I gave it back to Jojo," Gillian announced triumphantly, "before he left Chicago. He took it to California. I'll bet that crooked barber was working for Durkin. Maybe he *thought* Jojo gave it to me but he heard wrong. That's all there is to it."

"No," Shane said. "You've got the box." And took her eyes off the road for just a moment to level with Gillian. "They pulled Jojo's luggage apart. They combed the car he hired and put a dent in the driver."

"But no one could hurt Doc. That's a lie!" Gillian shouted. But Doc hadn't driven her to the airport as planned. He'd driven Jojo, and the next morning Jojo had said—what? That Doc wrenched his back!

Gillian was suddenly truly frightened. It was a conspiracy against her and all her guardians—and her guardians' friends! Nobody was safe—even somebody as big and capable as Doc.

"I'm scared!" she said, almost in a whisper, with her stomach feeling hollow.

"So am I, Gill, so am I!"

"You're not a bad driver," Gillian admitted somewhat grudgingly as four cars fought for two lanes in a tunnel and Shane steered expertly through the maze.

"Thanks," Shane said, "but where's that box?"

"You think Jojo would let me carry anything that a bunch of crooks were after?" She saw that Shane was yawning even at these speeds and in this peril that lay ahead and all around them. The deep hollows under her eyes were evidence that she had only dozed in two days. "Why would Durkin let me leave London if he thinks I've still got this box?"

Shane yawned again and said tiredly, "Because I'm a better actress than he thought I was. I convinced him that your guardian—Jojo—had called you at the Goldcoast from California."

"But he did!" Gillian interrupted.

"I know—they checked it out. And it was lucky for me he had called. I told Durkin Jojo had ordered you to put the box in your trunk and not carry it with you."

"So now Durkin is waiting in Pisa for me to claim my trunk and take it through customs? Then what? There'd be plenty of policemen and airport officials there. He wouldn't dare try to steal my trunk in a busy airport!"

"He won't have to steal it," Shane murmured. "I gave him your baggage check."

Gillian gasped, "Well, *that's* stealing!"

"Listen, would you rather lose the trunk or the box that seems to be worth more trunks than Marshall Field ever sold? And he'd have gotten it anyway." Shane's voice was steady now. "Besides, the box isn't in your trunk. I know where it is. You packed it in those butter cookies."

"Those cookies haven't even been touched!" Gillian yelled.

"Not by me," Shane agreed with a wry grin. "Nor by wise-guy Durkin or we wouldn't be here. You made one big mistake, Gill. Kids your age usually go for sweets, but you didn't eat your dessert on the plane out of Chicago—not one bite of it—"

"I was full! I was stuffed already! I never saw so much food in my life!"

"You left your candy bars at the hotel and you didn't eat Alitalia's cookies—you even gave one of those boxes away. Sure I looked in your purse, and I never saw such a collection—but I decided you liked to collect anything that was lying around loose—even those airline toothbrushes!"

Gillian stared at the backs of her hands and made fists again. Biting her nails wouldn't help now.

"Well, if you're so smart why didn't you give the box to Dobble—Durkin—in Milan? Why did you switch sides?" A terrible thought struck her. Maybe Shane had decided if the box was so all-fired important she'd get it and keep it for herself! But that didn't make sense. Shane could've taken the cookie carton as soon as she figured it all out.

"Does this mean you're on my side?" Gillian demanded suddenly sounding almost humble.

"I'm on *nobody's* side," Shane responded, "but I realized what a fool I was to trust Durkin after he took Cory—" She broke off, and Gillian shrieked, "Took Cory? Took him *where?*"

Shane was growing flustered, "I can't talk and keep my mind on this highway and these maniacs."

"Then stop the car!" Gillian ordered. "*There's* a knife and fork sign—turn in or I'll scream bloody murder!"

Shane turned in, parked, shut off the ignition, leaned back against the head-rest, and closed her eyes.

And Gillian, sweltering in the intense heat, waited almost breathless for Shane to speak. "We might as well go inside," Shane said, "and get some ice cream or a cold drink—no use frying to death while I try to explain."

The spacious restaurant had wide, panoramic windows overlooking a lush valley. Gillian marveled at the scene even in her misery. They found a small table and ordered. "A lemonade, please, and an iced coffee. *Per favore.*"

"All right," Shane began, studying the motif on the tablecloth. "I'll start at the Bartlett Hotel." Durkin had ordered her to doctor Gillian's hot chocolate with a strong sleeping aid. "I only gave you a fraction of what he *told* me to give. But you slept so long I got scared. I thought you had fallen into a coma."

Gillian's mouth dropped open. Doped! She could just as easily have been poisoned! "And Cory—?" she asked dully.

"I phoned him from your room. Durkin made me do it.

I said I'd found a hotel but didn't know the neighborhood, and asked if he'd mind checking it out with me. I told him you were asleep and would be for hours."

Of course. An innocent damsel in distress makes a pitiful plea to a gallant, gullible knight. "But Cory didn't even *know* about the box! Why'd they have to bother *him?*"

"Durkin thought you might somehow have slipped it to him. And he wasn't taking any chances." She went on. "Anyhow, we went to this horrible little hotel, on the edge of nowhere, and Dobble had two goons with him waiting for Cory—" She picked up her glass of iced coffee but set it down again untasted. "Cory caught on fast, though. He didn't know what they wanted but knew they weren't friendly and that you were somehow involved. He must have trusted me, though, because he slipped me your ticket and money for mine and said to find Budd. Believe me, I knew they wanted to search Cory, but I never dreamed they meant to keep him there. Gillian, I swear it."

"If they lay a hand on him," Gillian said, trembling, "Jojo and Doc and Budd and all their friends will make them sorry they were ever born."

"Right now let's concentrate on finding Camaiore," said Shane.

When Shane was sorting out coins to pay for the drinks, Gillian found herself listening with some understanding to the cashier who was talking on the telephone. "*Si, signore, due—ragazza, signorina—*" and a description of a girl and a young lady, which made Gillian's ears burn with interest.

She missed the next few phrases but caught, "You wish to speak with them? No?—but I can—" and the word *sud*, south. So the cashier was telling someone over the phone that two girls were headed south on the autostrada not too far from Genova—Genoa.

Gillian tugged at Shane's sleeve and whined, "Aunt Ethel, Aunt ETHEL! Can't we please try to ask how to get to Siena. I think we're lost!"

The cashier sent another flurry of words across the wires and *Siena* was among them.

Suddenly Shane got the message.

"We have a map in the car. We can find Siena, Josabelle," Shane said, falling easily into the role.

They meandered out of the restaurant like two properly lost tourists. Then Shane whispered, "Now!" and they bolted for the car. Within seconds their car roared back on the highway.

Gillian looked at Shane and Shane looked at Gillian. And they burst out laughing. "Josabelle!" Gillian said. "*That* was an inspiration."

"Oh, Aunt Ethel," Shane said, still giggling. "It's my real name, but Durkin doesn't know it. Nobody does— outside of Bethany, Missouri!"

"I'll never tell a soul," Gillian promised.

"You made a nice try," Shane said, looking solemn again, "but Durkin won't buy it." She pushed the accelerator to the floor.

# 13

Camaiore slept a late siesta in a valley of the Apuan Alps. Michelangelo had chipped at the marble of these mountains during the Renaissance. Gillian read from the map folder, ". . . the plainly visible areas of stark white are not snow or ice, but marble."

"Okay by me," Shane said. Obviously her mind was on other matters.

The houses they passed were still shuttered against the heat and sunlight. All had bright awnings or canvas curtains over doorways. Even shop windows were drawn shut.

A lone bicycler pedaled lazily along a tree-lined avenue and Shane followed him to ask directions. But he turned onto a narrow side street and vanished.

"Maybe Budd won't thank us for bringing trouble right to his doorstep," Gillian said, voicing a worry that had simmered all along the beautiful but crowded Italian Riviera beside the shimmering Ligurian Sea.

"He can handle it," Shane answered.

"He's not a football player like Jojo."

"I'm following orders," Shane said firmly. "Cory's orders."

Then she smiled. "I wonder if there are any survivors here. Sleeping sickness has conquered this town, I fear. If you see anyone stirring let me know." She drove slowly down a road under a mantle of trees, and Gillian peered anxiously through the shadows.

Budd, she knew, was somewhere behind one of these shuttered doors. But which one? She longed to stand on top of the car and call to him at the top of her lungs.

". . . We'll keep crawling and hope for the best." A minute later Shane braked opposite a couple of parked Vespas. Three boys, talking nearby, fell silent when they saw her.

"Can you direct me to the house of Signor Budd Greenburg, Americano?" They grinned and shrugged. One boy whistled.

Gillian said, "You're talking too fast!" In broken Italian Gillian explained that they wished to find Signor Greenburg from Chicago, Paris, *entiendez?* No understand; more whistles, more grins.

With the window rolled open to the heat, the car was unbearable. Shane mopped her face with her sleeve. "Maybe we can find the police station—"

At that moment a driver stopped his car beside the Fiat, inches away, hemming them in. He slid out the far side and fairly danced toward them in his excitement, chattering in Italian.

"What's his problem?" murmured Shane, suspicious. "Can you make out what he's saying?"

Gillian shrugged, but she was listening for a recognizable word. The stranger, dark, mustached, and handsome, was obviously upset about something. He waved his arms as he spoke, pointing eloquently toward the north.

"Hey, I think he's been looking for us!" Gillian said

suddenly. "He's talking about a uniform—I think he might be a policeman and he's apologizing that he's not in uniform. Oh, Shane!" In her excitement Gillian gripped Shane's arm. "He knows Budd! Wow, maybe he wants us to follow him—to Budd's house!"

"Then let's follow him," said Shane. "At this point, what have we got to lose?"

The police car screamed through the narrow streets with Shane keeping desperately close on its tail. They careened around sharp corners and made a U-turn that nearly sent them into a stone wall, shot forward again, and braked sharply for a side street marked, Le Silerchie.

"That's it!" cried Gillian. "I remember, Budd said—"

"Just hang on," Shane broke in. "I hope you like heights!"

The road, which had begun to rise gently past a little grocery, past slumbering mini-villas, past walls and iron fences and a shrine and past a gun club, was climbing steeply, turning, and twisting.

"Are you sure he's a cop?" Shane asked doubtfully as the town receded below. Following the man's example she "sat" on the horn at each hairpin turn in the road to warn oncoming traffic. "No one will ever believe our story," she marveled, "*if* we live to tell it."

They had arrived. Here at the top of the rise, an ancient shuttered Italian farmhouse loomed before them. But beside it stood a modern villa with balconies overlooking the valley. Its doors and windows were opened wide but somehow, oddly, *not welcoming*.

The policeman parked but left the motor running, and hurried to assist the girls out of the Fiat. His chatter was courteous and even apologetic, Gillian thought, though now the words escaped her, while he bowed and with a flourish motioned them toward the entrance of the modern villa.

Gillian was already racing up the marble steps and bolting through the door calling hopefully, "I'm here, Budd, I'm here!"

But there was no answer. Only the distant harmony of mariachi voices coming from a phonograph.

"Budd?" She looked around timidly. Across the room on a low table lay the giant Mexican sombrero she had bought Budd at Puerto Vallarta!

"You won't believe this," Shane said, coming in behind her, "but the cop took off like a flash. If he *is* a cop—"

Gillian hardly heard. She ran through the house calling into every room, "Budd? Hey, Budd . . ." But only the stereo responded. It finished playing "Las Mananitas" and now went into a gusty "Guadalajara," but the house was empty.

Gillian felt empty too.

"Where do you suppose he's gone?" she wondered aloud.

Shane took a look at her and said casually, "Maybe he's out stamping grapes or whatever they do here—besides sleep—or drive like maniacs—"

She trailed off into silence.

"Are you thinking what I'm thinking?" Gillian whispered.

A deep male voice crooned, "My dear, what are you thinking?" And the two girls wheeled to face Kurt Durkin, feet apart, hands on hips, filling the doorway.

"All right, kiddies, the game is over. Give me the box."

He was white-faced and unsmiling, and Gillian saw that Shane was right. His eyes had a crazy look.

She was shaking. But curiously she was just as angry as she was scared and somehow that helped.

It was the way he stood there, so almighty sure of himself. In Budd's house! Nasty, pale Dobble-Durkin, with Budd mysteriously missing! And Cory kidnaped? And Jojo hopelessly beyond call—

She swallowed hard and said, "*What* box?"

Shane shot her a warning look. "Tell him where we left it, Gill. Or I'll have to."

*Where we left it!* Gillian understood.

"We put it in a locker at Milan," she said. But her eyes wavered and all those late-night movies seemed to catch up with her. "And I swallowed the key."

But Durkin didn't swallow her story. "Give me the box," he repeated. Gillian and Shane stood motionless before the man.

Maybe if I rush him, thought Gillian, I can knock him off guard long enough to hit him over the head with something. She was panting. Durkin would get the box or tear her to pieces finding it. Was it worth it? And if she gave him the box, would he let her go? What would he do with Cory? Where, oh *where* was Budd when she needed him?

"Shane McLane doesn't appear to have had much luck in retrieving our stolen property," Durkin said levelly, eying Gillian. "Perhaps I will be more fortunate. Start undressing."

"Now wait a minute—" Shane began hotly, but Gillian waved her to silence.

"I don't mind taking my clothes off. But Jojo and Cory and Budd will murder this creep when they hear about it."

"Your friend Greenburg," explained Durkin, "is currently wheeling his way to Florence, he got a message that you're stranded there. Moore is safely out of the way. And Jordan James is in Durango. Your *new* friend"—he looked viciously at Shane—"will regret her change of heart if the two of you don't hand over that box. Now!"

In the next room the mariachis played happily on. And Gillian oddly drifted back to Guadalajara where Budd was pointing out a sign in their hotel, WISHING YOU A WARMY WELCOME! He'd put these records on to wish her a warmy welcome to his new house. But Durkin coughed and she came crashing back to the horrible present. Think! she told herself. Don't lose control. Think, think, think! What would Jojo do? Delay, that was one thing. Take the other side by surprise.

Behind her was a still unfurnished room and next to it, the master bedroom. She'd had only the one brief run through the house but she was almost certain the bedroom windows were wide and low . . .

"Okay," she said finally to Shane's puzzled glance, "Shane can search me. But *not* in front of you. I absolutely refuse, and if you want to choke me go ahead."

She had struck a sensitive nerve. Durkin drew back involuntarily. "I'm not going to choke *anyone*," he said flatly. "I haven't laid a finger on your skinny body and I won't *need* to. Because you'll turn over that box. You have no choice." He motioned toward the bedroom. "All right, get in there!"

Outside the bedroom an olive tree nudged the windowsill. Gillian rushed to the window to prepare an escape route. Shane grabbed her arm. "He's crazy, Gillian. Give him the box, please. If he has to search you, he'll kill us both for sure!"

"He won't kill us, Shane. Because we're getting out of here. Now let go of my arm!"

Gillian was halfway out the window when the door swung open. "You blew it," said Durkin, and flashed a wide, sinister grin. "You had your chance, and you blew it." And thrusting out an arm he pulled Gillian back into the room.

And then Shane came alive. "Don't touch her!" she screamed, leaping between them.

But Durkin was past reason. He dealt her a crushing blow that sent her sprawling to the floor. Now Gillian screamed and tried to run, but Durkin had her in a stranglehold, clawing at her clothes with his free hand.

She kept on yelling. She had scratches that cut deep but she fought against the gouging hands and bit a hairy wrist. Two steel-band arms encircled her. She kicked and bit again. "Let go of me, you big ape!" She was crying, spitting, and choking all at once. Then amazingly the arms slackened their aching grip and fell away. She had shut her eyes in her frenzy to get away from the beast that held her but now she opened them. Durkin's head was gone.

A second later she saw it wasn't gone. It was buried in a colorful floppy sombrero and Durkin was being asphyxiated by it as an arm held it tightly drawn against his neck.

"Budd!" Gillian yelled. "Budd! Don't smother him till we find out where he's got Cory!"

The mariachis now sang of far-off Zacatecas. "EEEE-yowwww!" She felt like whooping with them.

"Hi, *tesoro*," Budd said, with the most reassuring grin in the world. "Cory's okay. Shall I finish off this fellow now?"

The policeman, who was tying the limp Durkin's hands behind his back, grinned and gave Gillian a reassuring wink.

"Meet Brigadier Vitali," Budd said.

"We've already met," said Gillian, and smiled her thanks. "Do cops always carry ropes?"

"No," laughed Budd, "but he wasn't exactly planning on finding a maniac loose here. Actually, the rope is Febo's leash."

"Who?"

"Febo, your new dog. He's out in the car now, waiting to meet you."

"A dog!" Gillian never thought one day could be so full of news, bad and good. "I've never *ever* had a dog of my own before!"

But she was talking to herself now; Budd was kneeling beside a dazed and dizzy Shane McLane. "What happened?" she moaned.

Gillian knelt beside her too.

"This is Budd," she said. "Budd, this is Shane McLane. She's—a friend of mine."

"So where's this box that's caused all the trouble? And what's it got inside that's so valuable?"

Gillian couldn't speak for a moment. The policeman and one of his helpers were leading a subdued and still gasping Durkin away. His eyes were hooded and his terrible white teeth were bared but not in a smile as he fought for air. She was glad to see that he limped, and she rubbed the bruises on her arms.

"Well, what about it?" Budd prompted.

"I don't know," she said.

He gave her a startled glance. "You mean you've lost it?"

"I've got it but I don't know what's in it. Jojo told me to give it to Cory—" her voice trailed off. She looked guilty and asked, "Where *is* Cory?"

"He'll be here tomorrow—and so will Jojo—he thinks it's important to see for himself if you're in one piece. I think he blames himself for all the fuss. Anyway Cory's still groggy and pretty mad but he'll live. You can give him his box tomorrow—one more day won't hurt and we can share the big surprise, okay?"

Both girls nodded weakly.

Budd explained that Cory had been drugged but when he came to he'd managed to buy himself out of captivity—being a newspaperman through and through. Then he'd wired Budd to tell him Gillian and Shane were on their way.

"I asked Brigadier Vitali to keep an eye out for you, or you might have been in much worse trouble. Because you see, I got another wire soon after that sending me on a wild goose chase toward Florence. I'd probably be there now if it weren't for Mr. Vitali. He managed to intercept me and tell me you two were *here*. And of course I came rushing back to find bedlam. Speaking of which"—he smiled—"how do you like the place?"

"Oh," chorused Shane and Gillian, "we *love* it!" And Shane promptly blushed, realizing she hadn't been asked.

Gillian said, "It's the neatest villa *I've* ever seen!"

"It's the *only* villa you've ever seen." Budd pointed out. "But I may have to move—they told me this was a quiet neighborhood."

# 14

"A goodly crowd assembled on the balcony at 11:00 A.M." That was the way she would put it in her diary, with old Mary Ag the first to read it.

"The survivors assembled" might be better yet; though everyone, even Dobble-Durkin, was surviving. Durkin, Vitali had learned, had once served a prison sentence for molesting a child. This was why he'd tried not to lay hands on Gillian until there at the end when he'd gone a little crazy.

Doc Sawyers had recovered and was legally pinning Mattson to the wall. The Roudy Goudy and its owners were out of business. The barber and the maid were in police custody. And Kurt Durkin faced a battery of charges that would keep him occupied for many years to come.

"We were a motley crew," Gillian would write, or maybe, "We were eight at the unveiling."

It was better than a family reunion. Jojo, Budd, Cory, and Gillian were there, of course, and also Shane McLane, Brigadier Vicente Vitali, and Padre Tom, a priest from Chicago who was a long-time friend of Cory's and a sculptor and was chaplain of the jail at a nearby mountain town where he had lived and worked for sixteen years, and a dark, lively man who was the owner of a local restaurant in a one-time olive press—called El Paso which served what the owner hoped, Budd said, was Mexican food on Monday nights only. Budd had invited him because they were friends and because he thought Gillian, the old Mexico traveler and expert, would like him. She did. She liked the whole world with only a few exceptions this beautiful, beautiful morning.

"Okay, Gillian," Cory signaled, "where's this famous box?"

The murmuring crowd fell silent as she took Mrs. Burton's home-style butter cookies from her carry-on bag, and all watched intently as she gingerly peeled off the wrapper. Then she handed the dirty treasure to Cory. It was as tattered and worthless-looking as when it had begun its odd travels, but Cory handled it with special care.

When he lifted the ancient lid, they all could see there were loose papers on the top. Cory examined them closely. Then he gave Jojo an almost disbelieving look and said, "These seem to be pages from an old arithmetic—'sum books' they were called."

He explained that the pages contained problems copied out by a schoolboy long ago. In a queer almost choking voice he said, "Here's a sheet with a verse on it," and read aloud,

> *"Abraham*
> *his hand and pen*
> *he will be good*
> *but God knows when."*

Then he laid the papers gently on a table and removed the book from the box. It looked old enough to be Methuselah's diary, Gillian thought. It was handmade, with a faded maroon cover, and ruled pages. Cory was scarcely breathing as he examined the papers.

At last he said, "I don't know, of course—it would take experts on experts—but Mattson and Durkin *are* experts no matter how crooked—"

Jojo said quietly, "Well, just in case we've got our hands on something that really belongs to the whole U.S.A., could we let little Gill, who saved it, hold it once—maybe read us a line or two?"

She was feeling almost half scared to death, too nervous to remember to start at the beginning, so she opened the precious volume at the back and read aloud, with sudden, almost dazzling, understanding:

" '. . . I had this strange dream again last night. I seemed to be in a singular and indescribable vessel and to be moving with great rapidity toward a dark and indefinite shore . . .' "

She looked to the silent crowd. "It says: 'Washington City—14 April, 1865.' "

## ABOUT THE AUTHOR

ALICE CROMIE has had an exciting career as an author, journalist, and lecturer. She has been widely published in magazines such as *Look, The Saturday Evening Post,* and *Reader's Digest.* She is the author of *A Tour Guide of the Civil War,* as well as the mystery columnist and a book reviewer for the Chicago *Tribune.* Mrs. Cromie and her husband, Robert, who is nationally known for his TV program, "Book Beat," live in Grayslake, Illinois.